It was just a

Amalie closed her [...] the time of the mid[...]

"Northern Alaska," Jericho countered, parting her robe, his knuckles brushing the sides of her breasts. "An igloo."

"The ice walls are luminous." She rolled onto her back. "They glow with a pale, eerie light."

He moved over her, his weight propped on his elbows. "When I arrive by dogsled, the man offers me the use of his wife, as is the custom, but my preference is for the eldest daughter."

Amalie began to sink into the blissful aura of seduction. "I come to you, naked under the furs," she whispered. "I know you're waiting for me."

"You're so willing, so satiny warm," he said. "I find it so easy to slide up inside you."

"I've waited for you for so long," she panted. "But you won't stay."

"I can't." His hands covered her breasts as he surged between her thighs.

A cry tore free from her throat as liquid fire flooded her loins.... When it was over she took Jericho's face between her palms and made a soft promise. "You'll go away soon, I know. But until you do, I'm yours." She was careful not to use his name. He wouldn't know for certain that she was speaking not of their fantasy but of the truth.

Dear Reader,

Authors are often asked where they get their ideas. My answer has always been that my plots are pure fantasy, the characters complete figments of my imagination. Then, halfway through writing *Black Velvet*, I realized there was something familiar about the story.... Was it because I am a quiet and modest ex-librarian writing steamy pseudonymous romance fiction that likely scandalizes the folks back in my small hometown, and *Black Velvet* is about a quiet, modest librarian who uses the name "Madame X" to keep her bestselling erotica a secret from friends and family? Hmm...

Here's where fantasy splits from reality. Meek Amalie Dove meets Thomas Jericho, who is man enough to challenge her to truly become "Madame X." And when sparks fly, a BLAZE is sure to follow! And then another...and another... *A Touch of Black Velvet* will titillate you in October, and *Black Velvet Valentine* will heat you up in February. You could say *Black Velvet* is the beginning of a three-alarm BLAZE!

Gentle readers, bring your smelling salts. Adventurous readers— you know who you are!—proceed full speed ahead. And when you're finished—if your fingertips aren't too singed— drop me a line at Harlequin Books, 225 Duncan Mill Road, Don Mills, Ontario, Canada M3B 3K9. I'd love to hear from you!

Sincerely,

Carrie Alexander

Books by Carrie Alexander

HARLEQUIN TEMPTATION
536—FANCY-FREE
598—ALL SHOOK UP

BLACK VELVET
Carrie Alexander

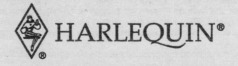

TORONTO • NEW YORK • LONDON
AMSTERDAM • PARIS • SYDNEY • HAMBURG
STOCKHOLM • ATHENS • TOKYO • MILAN • MADRID
PRAGUE • WARSAW • BUDAPEST • AUCKLAND

ISBN 0-373-25789-9

BLACK VELVET

1

An avian name suited Amy Lee Starling. She was a tiny chickadee of a woman with a plump bosom and bright eyes that darted to and fro in accompaniment to the quick, birdlike movements of her hands. Though Amy Lee had been known to preen behind her desk at the local high school, cooing and clucking at her students, she was thought by the islanders to be rather dowdy, with her drab, dark hair, muted colors and meek disposition.

Fluttery as she could appear, Amy Lee was also cautious in all things. Wide-eyed and silent as an owl, she kept her own council in personal matters, which was perhaps why no one on Bellefort Island suspected her of having a secret life. Not a single soul dreamed that Amy Lee Starling had taken a lover whose name she did not know.

AFTER QUICKLY REREADING the first two paragraphs of the story entitled "Tryst," Thomas Janes Jericho snapped shut the book, his long fingers splayed across the black velveteen covers. His suspicions had already been roused; now they were inflamed. Madame X was not at all what he'd expected. She was as far from the plain, mild-mannered woman who appeared several times as a character in the *Black Velvet* stories as he'd be from a Pulitzer if he went through with this damn article.

Jericho frowned, questioning his conclusion. In his experience, fiction writers usually put themselves into their work, be it intentionally or subconsciously, disguised or clear-cut. Therefore Madame X, the literary mystery woman, should have turned out to be a real-life version of Amy Lee Starling.

Instead she was a knockout.

Even more, he decided, observing the hoopla of the woman's publishing party with a cynical eye from his slouched position behind a massive potted palm. Madame X was a dream girl—a fantasy come to life. Norris Yount, publisher of the two *Black Velvet* volumes of sexy vignettes, must be thanking his lucky stars. If he'd called Hollywood to cast the part of the author of Pebblepond Press's astonishingly popular series of erotic short stories, Yount couldn't have chosen better.

Which made Jericho wonder if the pompous publisher had. Cast the part, that was.

Madame X was too gorgeous to be believed. She possessed thick blond hair the same shade as the brushed-gold links in her chunky necklace and earrings. Fabulous legs in shimmery, black silk hose. A figure to salivate over, displayed to slinky perfection in a backless, sleeveless, tighter-than-a-miser halter dress—in the signature black velvet, naturally. And her face was perfection: touch-me ivory skin; pouty red lips meant for serious kissing; long, slim nose; big sapphire eyes that somehow managed to look both innocent and seductive.

All in all, the quintessential Central Casting starlet, headlining in a production that at least one cynical observer was beginning to believe was pure artifice.

If this so-called Madame X had written even one

word of the *Black Velvet* books, Thomas Janes Jericho would eat Yount's wife's ostrich-plumed hat. With ketchup and mustard and relish.

Madame X, a statuesque five-eleven in her spike heels, tilted her head and leaned in closer so the bow-tied book critic from the *New York Express* could whisper in her ear. Batting her lashes, she responded in a breathy, husky voice pitched too low for Jericho to overhear. The critic simpered; the strained expression on Norris Yount's gaunt face relaxed into lofty satisfaction. He'd been hovering protectively at Madame X's side since introducing her to the party guests gathered in the vast atrium of the Rockdell Building, but now he clapped a hand between the influential *Express* critic's shoulder blades and went off to schmooze with someone else.

Apparently, pure artifice or not, Madame X's launch was meeting with success.

Scowling, Jericho pushed himself away from the cool stone wall and circled the edges of the crowd, now and then catching the occasional comment that rose above the trickle of the fountains and the usual drone of booksellers, critics, authors, publishers and a healthy sprinkling of the requisite glitterati.

A blond trophy wife whispered to a giggly girlfriend, "I already had a pair of black velvet evening gloves, so I put them on and called a limo...."

Straight from "Limousine Lover," Jericho thought, automatically categorizing the reference. *Black Velvet II.*

One of the Pebblepond Press PR minions was frantically hyping the product to a knot of sales reps mainly interested in the free booze. "The books are flying off the shelves. No, no, they're *zooming* off the shelves."

No accounting for taste, Jericho decided. Or a lack

thereof. And there was no accounting for how many hangers-on would jump aboard the publicity bandwagon, he realized as he spotted Lars Torberg, the six-foot-five, glacier-faced, B-movie action hero. Lars was staring across the room at Madame X, clearly fascinated.

A waitress with a cheese tray swept past Jericho and offered the selections to Kelly Ann Spofford, the infamously perky talk show hostess. Kelly Ann took an artful creation of goat cheese and black olives. "Golly, when you get right down to it," she said to her companion without missing a beat, "isn't it just smut?"

Mrs. Norris Yount gestured with a flash of diamonds and a tip of the brim of her flamboyant hat. "Perhaps, but it's hugely profitable smut, lovey."

Kelly Ann narrowed her eyes. "Forty carats?" she calculated. "Harry Winston?"

Jericho turned away, edging past the blue-haired, dumpling-figured psychologist who was known as Hollywood's favorite sex therapist. "I could make the *Express* list, too," she was saying, shooting visual poison darts at Madame X, "if I looked half as good as her."

A bearded Manhattan bookseller chuckled. "Gorgeous is as gorgeous does. Madame X's books are rocketing off my shelves."

Same old, same old, Jericho thought, breathing shallowly. Not even the atrium's mini–rain forest could clear air so thick with the fumes of envy, gossip and expensive perfume. No one seemed to care whether or not Madame X was genuine; all they could see was sex, scandal and dollar signs. Norris Yount could have trotted out Kelly Ann Spofford, Miss Spick-and-Span herself, and the party-goers would have oohed at her fall from grace, applauded her rise up the bestseller list and then reached for their drinks. They were as accepting and unquestioning as all brainwashed devotees of the cult of personality.

Artifice, Jericho repeated to himself as he glanced around the airy stone-and-glass atrium. He despised it.

The only guest who looked as discomfited as he figured he did—in fact the only guest who looked anywhere close to his image of the real Madame X—was the woman standing by the gnarled baobab tree, the quiet, dark-haired pixie dressed in soft layers of pigeony cream and gray. Actually, he realized as he took a closer look, she appeared to be so nervous she was out of place. Her eyes darted behind wire-frame glasses; a sheen of perspiration glistened on her pink cheeks and upper lip. She was clenching a plastic cup of red wine so tightly it was about to crack under the pressure.

A mail-room peon who'd snagged the invitation out of an editor's trash can, Jericho guessed. That, or a rival erotica author whose sales were dwindling because her own feeble public image didn't make the grade in these ruthlessly telegenic times.

Madame X's throaty giggle floated above the chatter, prompting the anxious pixie to scan the crowd. Jericho watched her rise to her toes in an attempt to see past the silver-maned literary lion who was explaining to the sycophants gathered around him why his magnum opus was taking ten years to write. When she began mumbling "Excuse me" and worming her way toward Madame X, Jericho changed his mind. A fan. The pixie was a fan.

He started to follow, just to see if she'd actually kiss Madame X's black velvet hem, but then caught sight of the top inch of Harry Bass's wild white curls and veered away instead. The *NewsProfile* editor-in-chief was making kissy-faced goodbyes with the trophy wife, abusing his lack of height to look down her ample cleavage.

Jericho grabbed Harry's arm and spun him away from the bottle blonde. "I want out of this gig, Harry."

Harry stuck out his pugnacious jaw and shook his head, making his jowls quiver. "We've been over this. And over this. We made a deal. Signed and sealed."

"I thought I could do it but I can't." Jericho stabbed a finger toward Madame X. "I mean, *look* at her. What else is there to say?"

Harry's eyes gleamed salaciously even though he couldn't possibly see the comely author through her throng of admirers. At five-four, Harry was nine inches shorter than Jericho and built like a fireplug, with a bulbous nose and a mottled, slabby face capped by a pure white fright wig. Of late, perhaps in retaliation for a recent rancorous divorce, Harry had been behaving like a sleazy, on-the-make bachelor, particularly when his ex-wife was in the vicinity. And since Rosie Bass just happened to be the editor of the latest edition of *Black Velvet*, she was definitely in the vicinity tonight.

"Photographs," Harry replied, chuckling. "Lots of sexy color photographs. I want to see skin."

Jericho rolled his eyes. When he'd begun freelancing for Harry, *NewsProfile* had been a weekly magazine featuring serious, in-depth interviews with newsmakers from the spheres of politics, science, art, finance. More recently, celebrity-of-the-minute profiles with artsy, full-page fashion photos and minimal softball Q & A's had ruled the pages. Newsstand sales had soared.

"Then you don't need me," Jericho said. Even though *he* unfortunately still needed *them*. He'd simply have to find another source of money for the last of the down payment he was trying to raise. Very quickly.

"We had a deal," Harry barked. "You reneging?"

"Look, Harry, you want a schlocky piece about how Madame X is reveling in the life-style of the rich and famous because she knows how to appease the stifled sexual appetites of the American housewife. Send Doppler—he'd love the research. Or Clarke. She'd find a feminist angle."

"I want you."

"Aw, Harry. Give me a break."

"Tell you what. I'll give you…" Harry narrowed his eyes and named a figure that nearly doubled Jericho's already generous fee. "I'll even give you a cover by-line."

"Since when is this a cover story?"

Harry chortled. "Since I got a look at Madame X."

Jericho scrubbed his hand across his face. Damn it, he was tempted. Paraphrasing Mrs. Norris Yount, this story might be schlock, but it would be hugely profitable schlock. And he had a use for the money, a use—a *need*—that had been festering inside him for longer than he cared to remember. Generally, he did his best not to.

Harry zeroed in for the kill. "Remember, you also get to choose your next three profiles." He'd previously bargained this additional perk down from Jericho's preference of five. "I won't even say no to that dog-faced environmentalist you're so keen on. So long as you don't expect many pictures."

Jericho groaned. "Two weeks on a publicity tour with Madame X, just so I can finally write about a person with something worthwhile to say."

"Look at her," Harry said. "I'd call it a win-win situation."

Jericho couldn't see past the gabbling admirers. "Shit," he said, knowing he was going to succumb.

"We've all got to shovel it sometime, Jericho."

"Yeah, and this party's knee deep."

Harry was eyeing a young woman in the standard Manhattan-cocktail-party sleeveless black mini. "That's your problem. All I see are lovely, lovely ladies."

"Harry, that girl's young enough to be your granddaughter. If Rosie catches you leering like that, she'll bite off your head and chew it to a pulp."

"Naw, she'd spit me out. Says I leave a bad taste in her mouth." Harry patted his white, Brillo-pad hair, purposely blanking the regretful expression that had appeared on his face at the mention of his former wife. "Anyway, Rosie who? I don't know any Rosie." He edged into the crowd. "I've got to learn this girl's name. I'll bet an alimony payment that it's Tiffany." He plunged into the crowd.

"Hey, Harry," Jericho called.

The short, barrel-chested editor looked back distractedly.

"Why me?" Jericho asked. "You know I hate these kind of assignments, so why, from all your staff, did you have to pick me to write the Madame X fluff piece?"

"Because you're the best."

Jericho scoffed. "Where's my shovel?"

"Okay, okay." Harry grinned. "Maybe because I don't want a fluff piece."

"What?"

Harry was being swallowed by the crush as the guests moved toward the table where Madame X was signing free books. Jericho saw the editor's white head bobbing up and down, but all he heard was a vague "…something stinks…" and then Harry was gone.

Yeah, Jericho thought, shouldering his way through the crowd. *Something stinks.* And it wasn't what he was wading through, it was what he was wading toward.

Madame X looked up from the open book an eager little helper obligingly slid under her raised pen. She licked her lips and smiled coyly at Jericho. "What's your name, darlin'?" she purred in a soft Southern accent, a lock of her golden hair swooped across one big blue eye.

He smiled tightly and prepared to ingratiate himself with Madame Fraud. Ever since his first paycheck, he'd been saving to buy a certain plot of exclusive oceanside real estate, and now that it was finally going up for sale, so was he.

It had better be worth it.

AMALIE DOVE WAS as nervous as an amateur performing on a high wire. Which was essentially the case, she supposed. Thank heaven Lacey, with her experience as an actress and model, was carrying the larger load. As long as Amalie didn't have to explain her continual presence and Lacey didn't have to extemporize too drastically, they might manage to pull off this charade.

Then they'd only have to repeat the performance on demand for the next fourteen days straight.

Good grief. Amalie's hands trembled as she automatically opened another copy of *Black Velvet II* to the title page and slid it over to Lacey. What had she gotten herself into? How had this terrible fraud come about?

So, all right, yes, she'd done it to herself when she'd consented to that first thrilling but un-thought-through publication of her initial *Black Velvet* collection. She'd then worsened the situation by chickening out and sending Pebblepond Press a head shot of her beautiful, golden-haired college sorority roommate, Lacey Longwood, instead of one of herself, when the publicity department had demanded an author photo for the new book. It had seemed a minor transgression at the time, or so Amalie had consoled herself. How could she have foreseen that such an itty-bitty deception would lead to the present gargantuan mess?

Amalie opened another book. Was there any way to get out of this now that things had gone so far?

There wasn't. There might have been at the beginning, if she'd had the nerve to speak up, but now it was too late. The plans were set, the tour booked. Ten cities in fourteen days, book signings galore and media interviews to fill in all the cracks. There was absolutely no room to maneuver.

Amalie Dove, the *real* Madame X, was stuck in a lie of her own making.

"What's your name, darlin'?" Lacey cooed seductively as Amalie slid her another black-velveteen-covered book. Amalie blinked and looked up from the diminishing stack. Although Lacey, bless her heart, had been playing the part of Madame X to the hilt all evening, not even Norris Yount had been the recipient of so much pure, unadulterated sugar.

"Jericho," said the tall, tawny-haired man on the other side of the table. "The name is Jericho." His voice was low, soft, lazy and…and *dangerous.*

Amalie shivered without knowing exactly why.

How ridiculous. Of course the man wasn't dangerous—he was a party guest. She recognized him. When she'd been separated from Lacey and shoved off in the direction of the indoor jungle, she'd noticed this guy prowling around the edges of the room like a cougar in a cage. She'd wondered about him because he wore a creased, cracked brown leather jacket over a plain white shirt and soft, bleached-out jeans, quite unlike the rest of the dressed-to-the-teeth guests. And she'd wondered about him because his expression had been so skeptical. But he certainly wasn't dangerous. Any qualms she felt were of her own making.

True, up close this guy looked *extremely* skeptical, even though he was presently making a halfhearted stab at friendliness. Amalie looked beyond the put-on smile to the cynical gleam in his sea green eyes and the belligerent set of his jaw. *Danger,* she thought again. An electric tattoo tickled her nerve endings as she sat up straighter, her senses sharpening instinctively.

"Jericho what?" Lacey said with an untroubled ease, scanning him from beneath her lowered lashes. She smiled, her red lipstick gleaming wetly. Amalie's gaze flicked from Lacey to Jericho. She'd quickly recognized Lacey's Marilyn Monroe expression, having once watched as it was practiced endlessly in the bathroom mirror while Amalie waited outside the door with a shower cap and a towel.

Most men melted under the full-force Marilyn, but this one stood firm. "Just Jericho," he said smoothly, and then leaned forward, knuckles resting on the tabletop as he looked deep into Madame X's eyes. "Isn't that enough?" With a demonic quirk of one eyebrow, he handed Lacey his own personal copy of *Black Velvet II* to autograph, making the action seem meaningfully intimate.

Very cozy, thought Amalie. Startled by the unexpected bite of jealousy, she caught her lower lip between her teeth with a quick intake of breath. While Amalie was pretty much accustomed to Lacey's effect on half the population, it might have been nice to have such a good-looking male gazing at *her* that way. Even once. But then, if she had, she might not have had reason to invent the fantasies that were presently pleasing scores of readers. Perhaps it was a trade-off.

A lopsided trade-off, Amalie decided, looking past the wire frames of her glasses to admire the table-height contours of the stranger's thighs. Embarrassing as it was to admit, she had kind of a thing for men's thighs—powerful, taut, solid thighs—and this guy's were especially thrilling, magnificently showcased by the faded blue-white denim of his jeans. Amalie almost grinned to herself. That could be why he wore them everywhere.

Lacey's gaze had lingered on Jericho's face. She smiled inscrutably and wrote in the book with a lavish hand. Amalie blinked foggily and gathered her wits in time to peer past her friend's elbow to check the inscription. "To Jericho," it read. "555-8192."

Amalie's gasp drew Jericho's gaze, but she was too horrified to notice that she'd gained his attention. Lacey autographed the book with the extravagantly swirly "Madame X" signature. Winking flirtatiously at Jericho, she blew the ink dry and started to hand the book across the table.

Amalie snatched it away. "You can't do that!"

"Am—" Lacey swallowed the rest of the name, remembering just in time that *she* was supposed to be Amalie Dove—at least to Norris Yount and the limited number of his employees who were privy to Madame X's true identity. She smoothly reversed herself. "Ah'm only bein' friendly, sweetie." The Southern accent was plastered on thick enough to spackle a pothole. "There's nothin' wrong with that, is there?"

"Yes, there is," Amalie hissed directly into Lacey's ear. "You cannot give out Lacey Longwood's Manhattan telephone number when you're supposed to be Amalie Dove, a.k.a. Madame X!"

"But look at him," Laccy whispered back. "He's adorable. A hunk and a half!"

"I don't care..." Amalie faltered as she recognized the truth, then swiftly recovered. "I do not care," she lied, "and that means *you* don't care, *Amalie.*"

Lacey sighed. "I suppose you're right."

Regretfully, thought Amalie, knowing she was missing out on more than a pair of great-looking thighs. She murmured a quick apology to Jericho and tucked the book with the verboten telephone number in the outside pocket of the satchel stowed under her chair. She brandished a fresh book from the top of the pile. "You don't mind, Mr., uh, Jericho?" she asked. "This book's just as good."

He looked curious, not appeased, but he didn't demand the return of his original. Amalie realized too late that while she might have prevented a catastrophe with the hasty book switch, she'd also provoked his interest—his potentially dangerous interest.

Her skin crawled at the intensity of his continued close examination. She'd wished only moments ago for exactly that, but now that his attention was on her, she had to look away. Then she couldn't stand the blind suspense of not knowing if he was still staring and she had to look back. Peeping up at him cautiously, her face hot and her bloodstream thrumming with adrenaline, she saw that Jericho's head was cocked. His eyes were narrow and unblinking, so pale they were eerie. He was a cougar again, as intent on her as if she, Amalie, was his prey.

That's your guilt talking, Amalie told herself. *That's your wild imagination running away with you. All he wants is an autograph.*

"Here you go, darlin'," Lacey said, and pressed her puckered lips against the title page, making a red lipstick imprint below her signature. "Real special, just for you, Jericho."

He glanced at the book and smiled, sort of. Amalie's racing pulse stuttered, then evened out. He was just a fan. Just a fan. *Please, God, let him be just a fan.*

But oh my gosh, may the devil take her to someplace truly wicked if he wasn't!

"Enjoy," purred Lacey.

Jericho tucked the book under his arm. "Now that I've met the mysterious Madame X, I'm sure I'll find her stories even more intriguing." He stepped away from the table, his gaze again straying toward Amalie.

Lacey gave him a shrug-shouldered, slit-eyed Marilyn smile and fluttered her fingers goodbye. Jericho nodded, but it was Amalie he watched as he slowly turned away.

Even though an unusually strong feminine impulse tempted Amalie to return his stare measure for measure, she averted her eyes. Whether or not he was dangerous, Jericho was a thoroughly attractive man, and by some miracle not one who'd been irrevocably awestruck by Lacey's looks. He'd struck a chord inside Amalie and it was reverberating through her, demanding something more than her usual demure response.

Then again, even if she dared, she was here under false pretenses. Unless she owned up to her identity— fat chance of that—nothing could ever come of furthering their acquaintance. At least nothing honest. Nothing polite. Nothing…tame.

The thought came unbidden: *Then why not settle for something wicked?*

Amalie shivered. Now, really, that was too much. It must be this prolonged exposure to erotica and game playing that had sent her inhibitions reeling; she'd do best to remember her position and rein in such wayward thoughts. She was a lily-livered author-in-open-hiding, not a femme fatale. She could dream up wild fantasies and even set them down on paper, but she would never dare live them. Such drama and glamour were for the Lacey Longwoods of the world, not the meek Amalie Doves.

Repentant, she tried instead to make herself unobtrusive behind the stack of books. Normally, with gorgeous, gaudy Lacey beside her, being noticed was the least of Amalie's concerns. So why had this call-me-Jericho guy been any different?

Peering over the stack, she watched the back of his head and shoulders—he had thick, straight, sandy hair, longer than the collar of the leather jacket that made his shoulders look a mile wide—as he made his way through the crowd.

Just a fan, just a fan, she repeated to herself. *Just a fan of the Lacey Longwood version of Madame X.*

She touched a curious palm to her cheek and found that it was warm. Had anyone noticed her overwrought reaction to Jericho? Had she managed to remain discreet despite the itch of animal yearning he'd provoked deep inside her?

Apparently so. Lacey was busy signing another book, flirting with a massive Nordic hunk of a movie star. No one was looking at the mousy assistant; all eyes were focused on Madame X, just as Amalie had planned.

Telling herself that she was relieved, she rubbed her moist palms on the outside of her thighs. She readjusted her glasses. She straightened the books. Then she leaned her chin on her hand and allowed herself to sigh a little over the spine-tingling allure of handsome blond men and what might have been...if only she'd dared to actually *be* Madame X.

"I WAS WONDERFUL as Madame X," Lacey said with her usual confidence. She shook back her hair and put out her hands as if she was accepting an award with the utmost grace and modesty. "I'd like to thank the members of the Academy—"

"Hush," Amalie cautioned, stabbing repeatedly at the Close button on the elevator's control panel until the doors finally *whooshed* shut behind them. Alone at last. She let out a deep sigh of relief and slumped against the marbleized interior of the elevator car.

Lacey kicked off her high heels, stretched sinuously, then slumped beside Amalie. "Tell me I was wonderful, Am. Stroke my ego. You know how needy us actors are."

Amalie told the truth. "You were wonderful. You were the perfect Madame X." A resurgence of uncommon emotion made her voice sound wry, and possibly regretful. "Much more impressive than I'd have been."

Lacey's brows arched. "I still say you could've pulled it off. Your eyes are divine and your complexion's lovely. A little makeup, a push-up bra, a new hairstyle—you could have reaped all the accolades for yourself."

"I would've died of embarrassment." Amalie tucked a short strand of black hair behind her ear. She and Lacey were total opposites. Whereas Lacey was a statuesque blonde with generous curves and oodles of exuberance, Amalie was slender and small boned, five-four if she cheated a half inch, with a gamine Audrey Hepburn haircut and a manner that could best be described as demure. Their only physical similarities were blue eyes—though Amalie's were almost dark enough to be called purple—and sound-alike voices that carried a lilting South Carolinian cadence.

"It might be good for you to come out of the closet," Lacey observed. "As the real Madame X, I mean."

"And have to perform for fans and the media, the unrelenting center of attention?" Amalie shook her head. "I'd just as soon give back the *Black Velvet* royalties."

"Not really?"

"I shudder to imagine how the islanders would react if I suddenly revealed myself as the author of two books of erotica," Amalie continued, still shaking her head. "You've visited my hometown, Lacey. You know how quiet and conservative Belle Isle is."

"To say nothing of—" Lacey lowered her voice to a sepulchral whisper "—*the senator.*"

"Please. I don't want to take the chance of even thinking about...the senator." Amalie glanced upward, searching for a security camera. Thank goodness there wasn't one. So far even the few, select employees of Pebblepond Press who knew that Madame X's actual name was Amalie Dove didn't know of her connection with the South Carolina senator with the same surname. If Amalie and Lacey were successful in their masquerade as Madame X and her unassuming assistant, they never would.

The elevator stopped at the penthouse floor, where Norris Yount's office was located. Amalie held the door while Lacey slipped back into her shoes.

"I wonder why Mr. Yount called you up here," Amalie said worriedly. She peered down the silent, thickly carpeted hallway. The lighting was low—discreet golden spills from the evenly spaced, frosted sea glass sconces. At the end of the hall a brighter square of light shone from the open office doors.

Lacey came out of the elevator smoothing her tight, panne velvet dress over her hips. "He probably wants to congratulate you on the successful launch of *Black Velvet II*."

Amalie bit her lip. "You mean you. Congratulate you."

"Y'all should be getting the credit, but..." Lacey shrugged. "Whatever you say, Amalie."

"Shh. Our voices may carry."

"Oh, sweetie, Norris wouldn't be able to distinguish between us even if he did overhear. Remember how your own mama would call our sorority house and sometimes mistake me for you? Your editor hasn't noticed the difference, either."

Not yet, Amalie fretted, knowing she was lucky that the editor she'd mainly worked with had recently left her job and been replaced by Rosie Bass. The original editor would've likely made the distinction between Amalie and Lacey right off, or eventually picked up on one of Lacey's miscues in referring to their supposed mutual conversations.

"Follow me," Amalie whispered, starting down the hall backward, placing one finger over her pursed lips like the librarian she was at home.

Lacey laughed and strode toward Yount's office, swinging her hips in the supermodel strut. "Norris, darlin'," she said, looking over the top of Amalie's head as the tall publisher appeared in the doorway.

"Amalie, dear," he responded, extending his bony hands, palm up.

Amalie flinched at her name but remembered to make way for Lacey, the woman the Pebblepond Press publisher knew as Amalie Dove. It was confusing even to her—and she knew the score. Still, her only recourse was to continue playing her part and pray that they'd make it out of New York with their convoluted, mismatched identities intact.

Lacey put her hands in Norris's and kissed his cheek. "The party was a great success, wasn't it?"

"You were superb," he said. "A real pro."

Lacey winked over her shoulder as she was escorted into the office. "Nothing to it. All I had to do was be myself."

"And a lovely self it is," Norris replied, slick as glass. A slight start of dismay as he acknowledged Amalie's presence was the only flaw in his polished surface.

Silently Amalie followed them inside, just as glad she didn't have to take part in the unctuousness of the cosseted celebrity author kiss-up. It suited her far more to play the meek, silent assistant, even if that meant she was overlooked by everyone except the keen-eyed Mr. Jericho.

"I expect the book tour to be just as successful." Norris seated Lacey on a stylish, cream leather sofa angled to take advantage of the magnificent view out the floor-to-ceiling windows. She murmured in agreement.

Amalie took one of two matching celadon green chairs. The lights of Manhattan sparkled below, so bright and numerous they managed to dim the stars above. Everything here was upside down and inside out from what Amalie had always taken for normal— the sounds, the sights, the food, the people. Even Lacey, so sleek and sophisticated compared to the small-town girl she'd been before she'd left college to try modeling and acting in New York. While Amalie found it all very interesting and stimulating, after two full days she was already certain that she preferred quiet, poky Belle Isle, South Carolina, and a night sky that sparkled overhead, where it belonged.

Norris Yount plucked a bottle of champagne from a sterling silver ice bucket set on the coffee table. "We must celebrate this auspicious occasion properly," he said, peeling the foil.

Eyes dancing with pleasure, Lacey held two crystal glasses at the ready as he popped the cork. "Why, Norris, darlin'! How did you know I adore champagne?"

"I suspected as much when I paged through your current collection of stories." Pink scalp showed through his thinning silver hair when he bent over the table to pour a third glass. He handed it to Amalie. "Miss—?"

"Longwood," Amalie said after a slight hesitation. "Lacey Longwood." She and Lacey had decided that it would be easiest if Amalie assumed Lacey's name for the duration. That way, should either mistakenly answer for the other, they could perhaps still salvage the situation.

Yount had already returned his attention to Lacey. "I'm thinking of the story where the chanteuse and the American soldier celebrate New Year's Eve with the purloined bottle of vintage champagne she'd smuggled beneath her black velvet cape...." He sat beside her, sliding his arm around her shoulders.

"'The Songbird and the Soldier,'" Lacey said, promptly naming the story. She hadn't minded that part of her Madame X homework. "I'm glad you liked it, Norris. I hope you shared it with your wife."

The publisher drew back; Amalie silently applauded Lacey's sangfroid. Norris recovered quickly and raised his glass. "Here's to *Black Velvet II*, dear Amalie. May her sales be high, her readers loyal and her critics astute."

"I'll second that," said a raspy voice from the doorway. Rosie Bass entered the room, brisk and trim in a midnight blue business suit dressed up with a satin tuxedo collar. Having known Rosie only via telephone until two days ago, Amalie had at first been hard put to connect such a throaty smoker's voice with the reality of pint-size Rosie. But the no-nonsense manner, sharp green eyes and sleek pageboy streaked with gray seemed to suit both the woman and the voice very well.

Uneasily, Amalie wondered again if the incisive Rosie truly believed that her reclusive Madame X had turned out to be a glamour queen like Lacey. Yet even if anyone at Pebblepond Press *was* suspicious, they were obviously eager to go along with the status quo.

"Don't finish your toast without us," Rosie continued.

Realizing that another person had entered the room, Amalie turned in her chair.

"The journalist from *NewsProfile* magazine has just told me he wants to be in on every triumphant moment of your book tour, Madame X," Rosie said. "May I introduce you to—"

Lacey rose gracefully, a pleased smile curving her full red lips. Adjusting her glasses, Amalie craned her neck for a glimpse of the tall male figure hovering behind Rosie. Her throat tightened.

"—Thomas Janes Jericho," Rosie concluded. "I imagine you'll come to know each other intimately by the time the tour is finished."

Jericho stepped forward, both fists thrust deep into the slash pockets of his jacket, his face arranged in a smile-that-wasn't-a-smile. An expression that Amalie, with a deep sense of foreboding, interpreted as a cocky "Gotcha!" smirk. She shrank back against the green silk chair, realizing that she'd been wrong—and right.

Jericho wasn't a fan. But he *was* dangerous.

2

One hot summer night Amy Lee Starling awakened from a restless sleep to feel the dank air draped like damp black velvet against her skin, so heavy her movements and even her thoughts were smothered and slow. Her body ached in a vague, dissatisfied way.

The glittering path of moonlight on the indigo water seemed her only avenue for escape. On a whim she shed the inhibitions of her day-to-day self and flew down to the beach, loose hair and fine lawn gown rippling in the wind off the ocean. She was revitalized. Her bare feet danced in the cool wet sand and her heart soared with dreams of dashing men and daring women, dreams of extraordinary desire. She yearned for something to happen…something unexpected…something wicked.…

The man who appeared out of the surf could have been a figment of her overwrought imagination: tall, solid, mysterious, dangerous.

But he wasn't.

JERICHO INTENDED to expose Madame X's carefully guarded identity to the entire world.

Suddenly Amalie was sure of that; her suspicion of him had been instinct and not imagination, after all. He wouldn't be the first reporter to make the attempt, but somehow she believed that he'd be the most persistent. And Rosie Bass had just freely delivered to him the golden opportunity—two weeks of constant proximity during the book tour!

Amalie took off her glasses and rubbed her eyes. She got to her feet, cleared her throat and said carefully, "This wasn't noted in Madame X's itinerary." While it seemed strange to use the Madame X moniker in front of Rosie and Mr. Yount, one point she'd stood firm on was that the name Amalie Dove would not be released to anyone, under any circumstances. Hopefully they'd remember that.

Norris Yount seemed startled that the quiet assistant would protest. He turned to Lacey. "I'm certain our lovely Madame X has no objections."

Lacey and Amalie exchanged worried glances.

"You agreed to media interviews," Rosie said.

"We've sunk a king's ransom into advertising," Yount stressed.

Amalie gritted her teeth as Lacey put her hand on the publisher's sleeve. "Of course you have, Norris," she cooed. "And I do appreciate it—so very much. I simply wasn't prepared to have a constant companion taking note of my every word and deed." Lacey fluttered her lashes at Jericho. "Whenever would I let my hair down if Mr. Jericho was always at hand?"

"I hadn't planned to follow you into your hotel room," he said. One corner of his mouth twitched. "At least not without an invitation."

"Oh, my," Lacey breathed. She appeared to be enjoying the predicament. Amalie couldn't imagine why—never mind the journalist's muscular thighs. Inviting their—*his*—presence was only asking for trouble.

"I'm sure Jericho won't be overly intrusive," Rosie

said. "He understands that we won't release your actual identity."

"I do?" he muttered.

"Then that's settled," Yount said at the same time.

Lacey nodded. "I suppose we can manage." She picked up her glass of champagne and started chatting about the tour schedule.

Jericho approached Amalie, who, rigid and silent, was clutching the curved back of the chair for support. "We haven't been introduced...."

Amalie slipped her gunmetal-colored, wire-frame glasses back in place. She usually wore contacts, but had felt the Madame X charade called for a more studious look. The glasses were quickly becoming more of a barricade than a prop. "I'm Lacey Longwood. Madame X's assistant," she said. The lie should come easier with each repetition.

"Mm-hmm." Jericho nodded his chin toward Lacey. "So then you'd know her real name."

Amalie tensed. "My lips are sealed."

Jericho glanced at her tight mouth. "I can see that."

Trying to appear unresponsive despite her unruly inclinations, Amalie looked down as her fingers sank even deeper into the padding beneath the celadon silk—a color that nearly matched that of Jericho's eyes. Her hands sprang up involuntarily; she shoved them into the pockets of her gray crepe dress. Jericho probably thought that the timid assistant she was so accurately portraying was an easy mark. He probably thought he was going to charm something incriminating about Madame X out of her.

Well, he didn't know he was dealing with the real Madame X! And while Amalie preferred to maintain a quiet composure in comparison to Lacey's vivacity— even if she wasn't doing it very well tonight—that didn't mean she was a pushover, either. If she had to, she could deal with Jericho. She might even best him.

Lacey tossed her long hair over her shoulder and responded laughingly to something the publisher had said. Jericho's gaze traveled up and down her impressive figure. "It seems pretty amazing, all things considered, that Madame X looks the way she does. I had a bet with my editor at *NewsProfile* that the mysterious Madame X was really a grizzled, cigar-smoking, potbellied hack from Queens."

Amalie was also watching her stand in, partly nervous about what Lacey was saying, a smidgen envious that she seemed so comfortable among these people when Amalie did not. How did Lacey do it? Even though her acting experience was limited, she'd slipped into the publicity-heightened persona of Madame X as easily as Amalie changed clothes.

When Amalie had first found herself sinking deeper and deeper into the quicksand of her denial of authorship of the *Black Velvet* books, she'd been too panicked to consider accepting her rightful role. Now, seeing Lacey having so much fun with it, Amalie had to wonder. What if...?

"Funny, huh, Lacey?" Jericho prompted.

Amalie blinked. "Uh, yes, I guess you could say..." Belatedly, she realized that he'd insulted her work. "Wait a minute. Did you say *hack*? I'd wager that you haven't even read the books, Mr. Jericho."

His white teeth flashed in a broad smile. "I read the good parts."

"The good parts?"

"You know what I mean."

"Unfortunately, yes." She clenched her jaw. "Perhaps you should do some research on the literary history of erotica instead of simply skipping to the "good parts." It might be wise not to comment on that of which you know little."

"A bit defensive, aren't you?"

"With reason," Amalie snapped, venting other emotions into an aroused offense. "It's apparent that you plan to do a hatchet job on Madame X and *Black Velvet*. I don't stand a chance."

Jericho's expression didn't alter, but some faint flicker in the depths of his eyes told Amalie that he'd noticed her slip. "Nothing the author or I can say will change your mind," she hastened to add. "You made it up before giving Madame X a fighting chance."

"Aw, come on, Lacey, lighten up. You've got to admit this is all too theatrical. I mean, *Madame X*? Who could take a pseudonym like that seriously?"

The name had seemed a little on the melodramatic side to Amalie from the beginning, but putting her own name on the books was out of the question—for reasons she intended to guard ferociously from media investigations.

"The pseudonym was taken from the title of a famous painting by John Singer Sargent," she explained. "The same painting was reproduced on the cover of the first book, so calling the author Madame X seemed quite suitable. It may be theatrical, as you say, but it's also intriguing. Most of the readers seem to prefer the mystery." She met his eyes. "Certainly to a grizzled, cigar-smoking, potbellied hack from Queens."

"You're eloquent in your defense of Madame X, but are you saying that this woman—" he gestured at Lacey "—is merely a performer hired to promote an enigmatic, and possibly less photogenic, author?"

"Of course not!"

Jericho laughed. "Just checking."

"What you're suggesting..." Amalie stiffened her shoulders. "That would be...misleading."

"No, that would be a bald-faced lie."

She had no rebuttal.

"It would also be commonplace. Publishing business as usual," Jericho conceded. "Nobody with a lick of sense believes that Martina Navratilova and Margaret Truman and Ivana Trump—"

Amalie chimed in. "And Fabio and Newt Gingrich—"

"Actually write their own novels," he finished. "Not to mention all those so-called celebrity autobiographies."

She caught herself up before they lapsed into camaraderie. "Then why must you be so determined to reveal Madame X's identity?" she charged.

He shrugged. "It's my job."

"Muckraking?" She sniffed. "Some job."

"Truth telling," he corrected with firm conviction.

"Truth as *you* see it," countered Amalie. "Isn't it possible that there are very good, very personal reasons why Madame X doesn't want to reveal her real name? Can't you respect her privacy?"

"Not when she..." Again, he nodded at Lacey. "Not when Madame X herself is going on a two-week, ten-city publicity tour. That's what I'd call an open invitation."

Recriminated, Amalie swung her head away so Jericho wouldn't see the distress in her expression. She clutched her arms across her abdomen, telling herself that the upset she was feeling was only distress. She could not handle the complications of a sexual attraction on top of everything else. And she certainly could not be looking forward to wrangling with this dangerously mesmerizing man!

Absolutely not. Why, accompanied by a snoopy journalist and the burden of a lie she must protect, she knew the next fourteen days on the road were going to drag like a hound dog under the Carolina sun.

And before they were up, her life would be changed forever—if Mr. Thomas Janes Jericho had his way.

JERICHO FINALLY FOUND a pay phone on East 43rd that worked. First, he'd call Lil Wingo to make certain she'd be available for an out-of-town assignment, then he'd call his connection at an East Hampton real estate agency to finalize the deal he'd been working on. Everything was going to turn out okay after all; he'd already picked up on a couple of clues about Madame X's true identity and he might even find a way to enjoy himself on this farce of a book tour as long as Little Miss Assistant was around to spar with. She was an innocent—though perhaps not entirely—but also unexpectedly tart and quick-witted and...

A slow, deep heat suffused his groin. Okay, and attractive. With her precise air of delicacy and those exotic purple-pansy eyes in a heart-shaped face, she was extremely attractive. On the upcoming trip, she could well turn into either an amusement or a distraction—or both.

Then again, she could also be made useful. He could lure her into performing as his unwitting spy.

Still holding the phone between his chin and shoulder, Jericho flipped open the cover of *Black Velvet II* to Madame X's lipstick mark, intrigued by the possibilities of the first inscription, the one the assistant hadn't wanted him to see. Had it been racy, maybe X-rated? Could it have been something even more revealing?

The pixie assistant had seemed more in charge than Madame X, but then he'd observed plenty of celebrities who let their assistants run the minutiae of their daily lives so they could concentrate all their own energies on maintaining the facade. It would be interesting to discover if that was the case with Lacey and Madame X, rather a night-and-day odd couple.

Idly Jericho paged through the book, intending to set it aside so he could make his phone call, until his attention was caught by a snippet of the prose flashing by: "She took him deep into her mouth."

Whoa. Blood drained from his head at a dizzying rate as he thumbed backward, needing to see what came next even though he knew what came next. Instead he was drawn to another passage:

The American soldier bent her over the straw bale, one callused hand between her shoulder blades and the other roughly stroking the curves of her exposed bottom. Fabienne's hips squirmed enjoyably against the prickle of straw. The coarse fabric of the soldier's gaping uniform was equally tantalizing as it scraped against her flesh. She arched her back, lifting her derriere higher as the young American thrust hard—

The telephone receiver dropped with a clatter. Jericho lost his place in the book, his fingers skidding over the velveteen covers as the pages accordioned out.

"I want you," the butler confessed.

"More," the woman in the black velvet mask demanded.

"No names," Amy Lee agreed with a whisper.

Breathing hard, Jericho slipped one thumb under the

waistband of his jeans; they'd suddenly grown tight. The book dangled in his other hand.

> The bride-to-be giggled shyly, her ripe breasts round and pink above the lace bodice her groom had peeled down to her waist. "We probably should have waited until after the ceremony."

Jericho laughed shortly, with some relief, and thrust the book away as if it were a poisonous apple. He'd read all this before, of course, and hadn't been so strongly affected. Had the images seemed exceptionally vivid because he now knew the author?

Madame X's golden good looks should have come to mind, but instead it was the assistant he thought of, Lacey, the dark-haired pixie with the nervous twitch and the quick tongue and the supposedly guileless, yet actually cunning, almond-shaped eyes. Strangely enough, he had no problem imagining her curled up in bed, blushing, secretive, scribbling down her fantasies in the middle of the night. And she *was* closer in demeanor to the Amy Lee Starling character he'd taken for Madame X's model—

Someone nudged him. "You gonna use that phone or what?"

Jericho's head snapped around. "Yeah, yeah," he muttered, pulling the receiver up by the cord and trying to remember Lil's number through the slowly fading blur of Madame X's erotic images.

By the time Lil answered—"Yeah?"—on the sixth ring, he thought he had himself under control.

"Jericho," he said.

"You sound funny. Sorta strangled." Lil's own voice was thick with sleep. "Got something for me?"

"Madame X."

"Whozzat?"

"The erotica author. If you haven't heard of her yet, you soon will."

"Oh, yeah." Lil yawned. "*Black Velvet,* am I right?"

"Yep. I'll need you tomorrow morning at the NBS network studios. Early."

"I'm shooting a thing tonight—arrivals at a new club. Brad and his new girl are supposed to show. I'll be staked out till the wee hours."

"So aren't you glad I woke you from your nap?" asked Jericho, stacking coins on the ledge beneath the pay phone to keep his hands away from that damn book. It was nearly as tempting as the real thing—and again he thought of the pixie first, even though she hadn't been the one enveloped in black velvet. Her hair was dark and soft, though, and her skin would be smooth and her mouth warm....

With an effort he dragged his thoughts back to the conversation with Lil, focusing on her habit of grabbing catnaps wherever and whenever she could. "Six a.m.," he said, fully expecting the groan that she provided. Still, Lil rarely turned down a lucrative *News-Profile* assignment.

She didn't disappoint. "Who needs sleep?" she scoffed. "I'll be there."

"Pack for Philadelphia, Detroit, Chicago, maybe Minneapolis. We leave day after tomorrow."

"Chicago and Minneapolis?" Lil's bedsprings squeaked as she rolled over. "March in the Midwest means winter. Hell."

"Buy yourself a muffler," Jericho suggested heartlessly, and he gave her the details for tomorrow. Lil grumbled and complained and hung up in the middle of his spiel.

Jericho looked up Debbie Howell's number in his

pocket address book, manfully ignoring *Black Velvet II.*
He fed the phone with quarters.

"Hello?" Debbie chirped, perky as a coffeepot even
at ten o'clock in the evening.

"Hey, Deb, how are you? It's Jericho." He'd gone to
high school with Debbie. She'd been a cheerleader
with a hankering for hoodlums. He'd been a hoodlum.

"Jericho! When are you coming back to the Hamptons for a visit? We can have a few drinks, go out to
dinner, see what develops—"

"In two weeks," he promised. "Now, about the Vanderveer property—"

Debbie giggled. "Are you interested in me or my
real estate license?"

"For now, your license," Jericho had to confess, honesty being his policy. It had been strictly fun and games
with him and Debbie, never approaching anything serious. Same with him and Lil. "Am I safe to assume
that the heirs haven't changed their plans to put the
place up for sale?"

"Last I heard, the Vanderveer cousins were still ar-
guing about splitting the silver and antiques. But my
best guess is that I'll be taking their listing any day
now. Have you come up with the down payment yet?"

"Most of it. I'll have the rest soon. Are you sure I can
put a deposit on the property before it's officially
listed?"

"Listen, these cousins are so greedy they don't give a
hang how I sell the place just as long as I get them an
excellent price. You must be doing pretty well to afford
a mortgage so steep," Debbie added with obvious curiosity. She'd lived on the "wrong" side of town, next
door to the humble cottage owned by Jericho's grandparents. As a teenager, he'd been sent to stay with his
maternal grandparents whenever he'd gotten in trou-

ble and his stepfather had loudly proclaimed to be disgusted by the sight of him. Jericho's mother had preferred to maintain the peace on such occasions by banishing her wayward son from DeWitt Parish's ultraexclusive East Hampton oceanside estate.

"Pretty well," Jericho agreed evasively. Nothing in his personal code of honesty said that he had to answer every question put to him. "So, it was good talking to you again, Debbie. I'm going out of town for a while, but I'll get in touch with you from the road in case anything happens on that listing."

"Don't worry, Jericho. You've got yourself a piece of the Hamptons pie if you're absolutely sure you want it." She sounded doubtful.

Jericho's smile was grim. Oh, yeah, he wanted it. He'd wanted it since he was sixteen years old and he'd overheard DeWitt telling Betsy, the morning after the incident at their stuffy country club, that he was through making allowances for her vulgar son, that Thomas didn't have the breeding or the social graces to ever fit in.

Jericho no longer felt the pain of hearing those words from the only father he'd known. Whenever the memory resurfaced, he told himself that he no longer even remembered how he'd felt at the time, and that it didn't matter anyway.

Over the years, such stubborn denial had tangled his motives until finally he'd convinced himself that buying the house next door to his parents' was simply his reward for a successful career. He didn't bother to analyze how DeWitt and Betsy Parish would feel when they discovered that the black-sheep son they'd done their best to forget had moved in next door. He didn't even acknowledge that he wanted to be there to see the looks on their faces when it happened.

Likewise, exposing the *Black Velvet* fraud to the gullible public was for him merely a means to an end. He couldn't let himself feel any sympathy for the blonde in black velvet and her wide-eyed coconspirator. If they were on the level, they wouldn't be hurt.

And if not...well, tough luck, Madame X. It was a big, bad, mean, dog-eat-dog world out there.

3

Amy Lee was mesmerized.

Her impulse was to flee to safety, but she couldn't move. Cold saltwater swirled at her ankles, dragging on the hem of her nightgown as she stood stock-still, toes digging into the wet sand.

The man who'd seemed to come from the sea wore nothing but a pair of wet, clinging cutoff jeans. Moonlight bathed the slick contours of his bare chest, limning the sculpted muscles like a statue under a spotlight. *Except he's real,* Amy Lee thought in amazement, staring as he walked toward her, his face severe, his body exuding raw male power. Her gaze dropped; her eyes widened. The cutoffs were slung low across his narrow hips, frayed threads at the hem glued to the flexing muscles of his strong thighs. Wet denim only enhanced his blatant state of arousal. He was ready, she thought, her mind racing on adrenaline. He was aroused...by *her?* She opened her mouth to speak—possibly to protest.

Now an arm's length away, he stopped her with a look. "Don't," he said. "No words. No names."

THE ROOM-SERVICE WAITER gaped past the open bedroom door as if he'd never seen thirty-eight inches of bare, crossed legs before. Unconcerned, Lacey sat in front of the dressing table mirror brushing her golden hair, a flimsy, black chiffon robe split almost up to her waist, her red lacquered toes curling and uncurling with each stroke of the hairbrush.

Amalie signed the bill, added a tip even though a case could be made that Lacey had already been generous enough, and then pointed the happy waiter toward the door. At least they'd be ensured good service once he reported this incident to the rest of the men on staff.

Not that Amalie had any complaints with the service up to now. Pebblepond Press had booked her and Lacey into a luxurious suite in a pricey midtown hotel. It had two bedrooms with matching baths, a fancy rose-and-green sitting room and a gratis minibar stocked with everything from champagne to litchi nuts. There were fruit baskets lavish enough for Carmen Miranda, exotic floral arrangements in every room, hot-and-cold running bellboys on tap.

Apparently Norris Yount wanted very badly to keep the *Black Velvet* wellspring flowing. Amalie smiled to herself. All this was a strange and new experience for her, but one she was finding rather enjoyable—at times. The times she could forget that the entire situation was predicated by her lie about Madame X's identity.

Lacey wandered over to the breakfast table. "It's warm."

Amalie nodded. "It just arrived."

"I mean the newspaper." Lacey held up a crisp copy of the *New York Express.* "They've ironed it." They looked at each other and laughed.

"Did someone forget to tell them that we're only two little small-town nobodies from South Carolina?"

"Nobodies?" Lacey plucked a strawberry from a silver bowl. "After last night, sweetie, we're surely more than that! Wouldn't surprise me if we're front-page news." She popped the plump berry into her mouth and rolled her eyes with pleasure.

Amalie could not be so cavalier about Madame X's growing fame. She snatched up the newspaper and flipped through it to find the book section's feature article on the public debut of Madame X. There was also a review of the new book—and it was a rave.

"Oh, gosh, listen to this, Lacey. 'The *Black Velvet* books have become instant classics of erotic literature....'" Amalie skimmed the column. "'With a deliciously naughty contemporary flair, Madame X tempts the discriminating reader into a decadent world of sensual delight....' Wow! And there's a picture of you."

Lacey squealed and grabbed the paper. The photo was a companion to a gossipy sidebar about the party; it depicted Lacey leaning flirtatiously into the broad chest of Lars Torberg, the action-movie star. She was identified as "the mysterious Madame X, revealed at long last."

Dazed, Amalie sank onto a rose brocade love seat. "Imagine—me, reviewed in the *New York Express*."

Lacey pulled a chair up to the room-service table and reached for the coffeepot, all without removing her avid gaze from the newspaper. "We've come a long way, baby."

"Too far and too fast, as far as I'm concerned," Amalie said. She hadn't intended for any of this to happen when she'd taken a two-paragraph fantasy from her private journal and written her first full-fledged erotic short story in pencil on notebook paper, strictly for the amusement of her college sorority sisters.

Six years later, the print run of the initial *Black Velvet* book had been modest, though the book had eventually sold out. Amalie had been flush with just enough pride to sign a contract for a second collection. Figuring herself to be safely anonymous, she hadn't anticipated the consequences.

Even before its official release, the advance sales of *Black Velvet II* had exploded beyond all expectation. As soon as the book was on the shelves, reporters, moral watchdogs, gossip columnists and the public in general had begun debating the secret identity of Madame X.

Amalie had begun to fear for the peace and quiet of her anonymous life-style. She worried that every stranger who appeared on the island was a reporter bent on hunting her down. She dreaded the reaction of Senator Dove's electorate if she was exposed.

Lacey stabbed one finger at the newspaper. "They're still speculating about Madame X's real name. I told you they wouldn't be satisfied without a full introduction."

"It's impossible." Amalie wouldn't budge on that point, and fortunately the Pebblepond PR staff felt that maintaining the mystery would be good for sales. "You know I can't come clean, especially now that I've out-and-out lied to members of the press about not being the author. Look at how the author of *Primary Colors* was vilified once he admitted the truth." The guilt of what she was doing ate at her, but it was nothing compared to what she'd go through if the truth was commonly known. She thought of Jericho's hard eyes and cynical mouth, and how he'd like to see her squirm.

Luckily, Lacey considered the situation to be all in good fun, and beneficial for her career as an actress, as well. "All the more attention for me," she said with a shrug and a smile.

"We have to talk about how we're going to handle the *NewsProfile* reporter while we're on the road," Amalie noted worriedly. "He already suspects something. I wish I could stop him from coming along."

"Oh, Am, I'll take care of him," Lacey said breezily. "It should be enjoyable."

"He's going to ask a million questions."

"So I'll think up a million answers. You know me." In acting class, Lacey had excelled at improvisation.

Which also worried Amalie. "It's best to keep your answers simple. Easier for us both to remember and less chance of tripping up later."

"Mmm," Lacey purred. "Maybe Jericho will catch me if I do."

Amalie shot her a look. "I thought you were interested in Lars Torberg."

Lacey winked. "How long did you say this Madame X gig will last? I do enjoy having handsome men worship at my feet."

"The book tour can't be over fast enough," Amalie muttered, grouchy at the thought of Lacey's likely conquests, Jericho included. The sooner Madame X and her racy books faded into obscurity the better for all involved, right? She frowned. Yes, right, absolutely right. Her reaction to Jericho yesterday had been a freak occurrence, totally out of her usual bounds. Now that she'd gained some distance, she had a clearer head.

Lacey started to quote from the article. "'Madame X dazzled the guests in a slinky, black velvet dress. Her voluptuous presence perfectly suited Norris Yount's newest golden-girl celebrity author.'" She flung out her arms, scattering the newspaper across the plush green carpet. "Does that mean I'm fat, but sexy?"

"I think it means that you made another conquest." Amalie sighed and picked up the sheets of newsprint, smoothing and rearranging them as she went. Lacey had never had a problem attracting guys, but she was so ingenuous about it that normally Amalie could only smile at her friend's enthusiasm.

Lacey ate a spoonful of strawberries and cream. "I'll never be a supermodel unless I lose ten pounds." She stroked her hip. "Maybe fifteen."

"You're perfect. You're gorgeous. Anyway, you don't have to be skin and bones to be an actress."

"Oh, yes, you do. They say the camera adds ten pounds." Lacey brightened. "Still, the casting directors are sure to remember me once I'm famous as Madame X."

"But you'll have to give them your real name," Amalie said doubtfully. They hadn't really worked out the logistics of life after Madame X.

Lacey shrugged. "I wouldn't mind."

"I suppose the people at Pebblepond Press who know you as Amalie Dove might assume that Lacey Longwood is a stage name. But then they'll wonder what *my* name really was—if they remember your mild-mannered assistant at all once she's gone, that is." Amalie shook her head. "We should have thought this through."

"Or I could just retire on my renown as Madame X. I wouldn't mind that, either." Lacey added a sugar cube to her coffee cup. "You keep producing bestsellers and I'll keep basking in the glory."

"Lacey…I can't promise I'll *ever* write another *Black Velvet* book." Amalie hesitated. "This may turn out to be our—your—fifteen minutes of fame. And that's it." In fact, that was exactly what she was beginning to count on.

"Don't worry, sweetie, I was only teasing. I'm not expecting a run to rival *Cats*." Lacey took the coffee cup and pushed herself away from the table. Beneath her more outlandish airs was a good amount of practicality. "It'll probably be a miracle if I even make it to off-off-Broadway, so it's not very likely that anyone at Pebblepond Press will ever question our little con game." She urged Amalie toward the table. "Now, you eat some breakfast while I get dressed. After that description in the *Express*, the people at *Manhattan Morning* are expecting a bombshell. I've got a lot of work to do on my hair and makeup."

THE MADAME X SEGMENT on *Manhattan Morning*, a news, weather and entertainment show, was scheduled to last six minutes. Which seemed like a lifetime to Amalie as she observed from the darkened sound stage, but Lacey, comfortably ensconced in an overstuffed armchair on the brightly lit set, appeared to be taking her first live television interview in her high-heeled stride.

"The *Black Velvet* books are erotica, not pornography, Kevin," she said to the square-jawed host, remembering to hold the book face out and right side up as she turned to the camera and gave it her best Marilyn. Her hair was molten under the spotlights.

"Is there a difference?" the host said with a leer.

"Of course." Lacey smiled gently and looked toward the audience. "Erotica is literate, sensual, satisfying. And great fun! *Black Velvet II* is as delicious as a box of bonbons, ladies—but it has no calories!" Titters scattered through the studio audience.

In the shadows, Amalie twitched when a deft male hand touched the small of her back. "Is that true? Are you on the *Black Velvet* diet?" whispered an accompanying suede-soft male voice, making her scalp tighten and her follicles tingle. A faint scent of lime and leather lingered on the air. "And here you're already such a slip of a girl."

Stepping away, Amalie cast a wary sidelong glance at Thomas Jericho. He was wearing the white shirt and jeans again, with the same battered jacket slung over one shoulder. Although he carried no notebook or tape recorder, she assumed that everything she said was on the record.

"I suppose you can't understand how anyone would take Madame X's book seriously," she groused, her testiness at odds with the curious pulling warmth flowing through her body. She wasn't usually so sensitive, but Jericho seemed to have a natural talent for getting her back up.

He grinned. "Yeah, serious as a frilly box of bonbons."

He doesn't know he's insulting the real author, she reminded herself. "Well, how many books have you published, Mr. Big-time Journalist?" she asked impudently, hands on hips. "Maybe if you were on the bestseller list you could be interviewed by Kevin Kincaid, too."

Someone with a clipboard shushed them, giving Jericho an excuse to move in closer. "And have to follow the I Married an Alien act?" he whispered. "No thanks. I'll pass. Even though I have written a book."

She laughed softly. "What? *A Hundred and One Sneaky Reporter Tricks?*"

"Don't hate me because I'm inquisitive," he jested.

They both turned back to the studio set. Madame X reacted with aplomb even when the smirking host read a titillating snippet from the book; she suggested that he might need to liven up his own love life and laughed along with the audience when the host asked for her telephone number. One of the cameras zoomed in for a close-up as she succinctly turned him down, offering a free book in compensation.

"She's a natural," Jericho commented.

Madame X's dark-haired assistant nodded.

"But I still don't believe she wrote the book. She's too perfect for the role. Too beautiful."

"Oh, well, there's proof for you," the assistant retorted with a toss of her head. "The dumb-blonde prejudice." Though her voice was certain, even in the dim light Jericho could see that her eyes had narrowed to indigo crescents rimmed with feathery black lashes as she cautiously divided her attention, her gaze flicking back and forth between him and the set. The inappropriate amount of tension that radiated from her tugged at his suspicious nature.

There was definitely something fishy about Madame X and her overly protective assistant.

True, he had no proof other than hard-boiled cynicism and an aroused journalistic instinct. But one way or another he'd get enough evidence to write an exposé for *NewsProfile*. He had two weeks to catch Madame X or one of her entourage in a mistake that could lead to the truth. And there was no reason not to start prying immediately.

He touched the assistant's arm. "Now, then, I might be persuaded to believe that you're the author of *Black Velvet II*...uh, Lacey, is it?"

He was disappointed when her only response was the almost imperceptible tightening of her sexy little body, and even that wouldn't have been noticeable if he hadn't been touching her. She pulled away, crossing both arms tightly across her abdomen in a textbook defensive posture, though an outraged denial would have been more telling. Even a gasp might've done. Now he'd just have to keep on nettling her until he struck a more obvious nerve. He shrugged. A guy had to do what a guy had to do.

Her voice was as brittle as her composure. "I will not dignify such ridiculous tripe with an answer."

She spun on her heel and stalked off to confer with the *Black Velvet* triumvirate: Rosie Bass, the savvy editor Jericho already knew well enough to be certain she'd let nothing slip; Minette Styles, Pebblepond's gung-ho publicist; and the steely brunette who'd been introduced as a literary agent. The publicist might be a source in her overeagerness, but still his best possibility was the assistant, a woman obviously untutored in the game of artifice. She was so brittle that cracking her would be child's play.

Kevin Kincaid wrapped up the interview with Madame X and the audience applauded enthusiastically. Jericho picked his way through the snakes of cable coiled around the darkened stage, intending to find his photographer. Lil Wingo was destroying the day-old buffet in the green room. Cameras were strapped across her lanky torso like bandoliers, appropriately enough since she was a bandito with a zoom lens and wielded her Hasselblad as if it were a six-gun.

"Don't eat that," Jericho warned when Lil reached for a tub of what might be cream cheese. "It's green."

"So were the deviled eggs and I ate most of them," she said, spreading the cheese on a bagel with the back of a spoon. Squinting at Jericho from beneath thick sable bangs, she bared her teeth and took a huge bite.

Jericho winced. "I'll never kiss you again."

"Hah!" Lil held the bagel between her teeth and reached covetously for the fruit bowl. "Like I'm asking you to."

Out of town together on assignment, they'd occasionally lapsed into a we're-stuck-here-in-the-back-of-beyond-so-why-not-share-the-bed arrangement, then lapsed out of it when they got back to New York and remembered that they liked working with each other too much to be lovers. Jericho knew that Lil professed a deep, abiding love only for her cameras; Lil knew that Jericho was too twisted into knots inside to trust any woman with his wounded heart—but told himself that the only reason he wasn't in a serious relationship was because of his peripatetic life-style.

"If you've finished your salmonella poisoning, I think we can go," Jericho said. "Unless you need more frames of Kevin Kincaid's good side?"

"Think he'd bend over?" Lil snorted, separating cherries and melon balls from blackened banana slices and gobs of mushy kiwi. "That clown already stuck his jaw into half my shots." She'd photographed Madame X arriving by limo, getting reglamorized in the makeup chair, and in a zillion fakey, preshow poses with Kincaid doing his best to upstage his guest. Some men just didn't like women who were prettier than they were.

"Share a cab?"

"Nope." Lil stuck a muffin in the pocket of her baggy chinos. "I'm gonna scout the halls for a while. Maybe sneak onto a few sound stages, catch Kelly Ann Spofford chewing out a cameraman."

Jericho checked his watch. "Don't forget the book signing at one and the reading at seven."

Lil yawned. "Hey, I can catch a nap in between."

THE SUPERSTORE book signing went smoothly. Lacey was skilled at chatting with Madame X's fans, and so familiar with the *Black Velvet* stories that she could dis-

cuss even the pickiest of details with the most enthusiastic of readers. Some of them, clearly believing that
Madame X must be an expert, began asking for tips on
spicing up their love lives. Several got specific enough
to make Amalie blush, but Lacey responded easily, un-
abashed. Once again, Amalie thanked her lucky stars
that she wasn't in the Madame X hot seat herself.

Her relief deepened when they were escorted to a
smaller independent bookstore for a scheduled reading of one of the *Black Velvet II* stories. Amalie had en-
tertained doubts about the wisdom of the event, but
Lacey swore she was looking forward to the chance to
employ her talent for dramatics.

A bespectacled man in suspenders, the owner of the
shop, swept Lacey away to prepare for the reading.
Amalie looked around the wood-paneled, multilevel
room, feeling lost despite the familiar cozy, bookish
atmosphere. She'd stayed close to Lacey's side all day,
ready to salvage any awkward situations that might
come up. With the exception of Jericho's continual,
watchful presence, everyone they'd met seemed to accept Madame X at face value. Even other journalists
who'd been granted short interviews in between the
signing and the reading hadn't forced the issue when
Lacey laughingly refused to supply her real name. All
in all, Amalie was amazed that their charade had been
so successful. Thus far.

She took one of the folding chairs scattered among
the bookshelves skirting the edges of the main room.
The leather club chair on the wide landing midway up
the staircase was meant for Madame X. Already the
choice spots on the chairs and benches gathered before
it were filled with eager fans. Although most of the
loyal *Black Velvet* readers were women, the early evening crowd was at least half-male. Amalie wondered

tiredly how much Lacey's photo in the *Express* had to do with that.

She fingered the soutache trim of her bolero jacket, taking a moment to rest her eyes as she thought ahead to dinner with Rosie Bass and the rest of the Madame X team, and then finally their return to the hotel. It had been an exceptionally long day. Amalie wasn't used to the hectic New York pace.

The audience buzzed as Lars Torberg arrived, taking a reserved seat at the front, almost at Madame X's feet. Amalie forced her eyelids up as someone settled into the chair beside hers. The bookstore was filled to capacity.

"Now this I'm really looking forward to," said her new neighbor.

Amalie was suddenly filled with dread. "You again!"

Jericho looked at her and smiled. "Me. Again." He sat back, self-satisfied, making the metal chair squeak. "And for the next two weeks, too, so you'd better get used to me."

Amalie's spine stiffened. Suddenly she was wide awake, jets of alarm shooting through her bloodstream. "Shouldn't you be up front, near Madame X? I imagine you don't want to miss a single word."

"I'm more interested in observing the reaction to her reading."

Why did Amalie think he meant *her* reaction, specifically? Because he was staring again? Fixing her with those lazy, leonine eyes of his?

She faced forward, pink cheeked, emotions befuddled, her squelched libido stirring stubbornly to life. Heaven help her, it felt good to flirt with the danger Jericho represented. It felt good to be so alert—so *alive*.

"Do you know which story she's reading?"

"'Black Vel—'" Amalie stopped abruptly. Oh, no, oh, no, this was terrible. How could she possibly sit meekly beside Jericho as Lacey read aloud a tale of the explicit, anonymous encounter two masked lovers enjoy on a balcony in the midst of a masquerade ball? Surely that was too much to ask of anyone.

Swallowing dryly, she stared down at her fingers, laced tightly together in her lap. "'Black Velvet Mardi Gras,'" she whispered. The tremble in her voice was so slight that surely Jericho had missed it.

He leaned forward, elbows on his knees. "Yep. I'm *really* going to enjoy this."

Amalie moaned softly.

"Shh," he said, "we're missing the introduction."

Lacey accepted the generous applause and, after a bit of banter, smoothly launched into the story, her voice low and husky, but still carrying to every book-filled nook of the room. Amalie took a deep breath and closed her eyes. Except for jumping up and racing out of the bookstore, total denial was her only recourse. She wouldn't acknowledge Jericho's presence beside her, she wouldn't look at him, she wouldn't even peek at him. Sternly she adjusted her glasses, forcing herself to completely block him out of her consciousness. As far as she was concerned, he'd ceased to exist. Nope. Not there. *Bye-bye, Jericho. You're gone. Vanished. Vanquished. Vaporized.*

"The velvet black-and-white harlequin's mask she wore covered all but her full pink lips," Lacey read. "It was a mouth so ripe and decadent, so ready to be debauched, that the blood of her hooded, masked partner sang with anticipation as they waltzed around the candlelit ballroom."

Amalie tried to zone out. She screwed her eyes shut even tighter and crossed her legs, thinking about the

Dewey decimal system. About the clauses and sub-clauses of her eighteen-page publishing contract. About being audited by the IRS.

She sensed a whisper of movement. Was you-know-who looking at her again? The hair on her arms prick-led.

"...Below, the ballroom was ablaze with the light of a thousand candles. The masked woman turned away from her partner and leaned over the wrought-iron railing, admiring the swirling kaleidoscope of colorful dancers. She tossed a flirtatious glance over her bare shoulder. The man in the hooded cape and sparkling, gold-sequined lion mask stepped from the shadows. His arm went around her waist. 'Stand just as you are,' he whispered coaxingly. 'Let me lift your skirt.'"

Amalie's eyelids quivered; she *knew* what's-his-name was looking at her. And Lacey's words—*her* words—were impossible to ignore. The pressure of the situation built inside Amalie; her body felt warm and full, pulsating with need, ready to burst into flame.

Lacey continued. "'They will see,' the woman said, though in truth her protest was only halfhearted. This was Mardi Gras, after all, the only time of the year she gave herself permission to be wicked...."

The assistant recrossed her legs, blissfully unaware, as far as Jericho could tell, that his eyes had not left her. He watched her nervous fingers trace the ridges of trim on her jacket and wondered if she realized that it looked as though she was caressing herself. He stifled a groan, his lungs banded in steel.

She bit her lip and shifted on the chair, causing the jacket to gape. With an aching hunger he studied the curve of her breast and the bump of a hard nipple pressed against the thin silken shirt. And then he knew: there was a secret voluptuary locked inside Madame X's demure little assistant. Perhaps even one who'd already found a safely anonymous outlet.

"The rustle of the masked woman's taffeta skirt as it was raised and the throaty purr she made when his fingertips touched her thighs were the most erotic sounds he'd ever heard. Her flesh was warm and soft, plump where it was squeezed by a red lace garter...."

Jericho let himself sink into the seductive spell cast by Madame X's words. As he gradually became attuned to the responses of the assistant's body beside his, so close the temptation to reach out was excruciating, he entirely forgot to maintain his objectivity. He concentrated only on her, absorbing her tension, welcoming her heat. He imagined that he could count each beat of her heart and anticipate the quickening of her breath as Madame X read on and together they wound tighter, reached higher, came closer....

"...The long, full skirt fell around them, disguising their illicit movements from the eyes of the revelers. The masked woman wrapped her gloved hands around the iron railing, bracing herself as her partner pushed his leg between hers and stroked his palm down the seam of her buttocks to find the molten warmth seeping onto her thighs. His fingers slid deep inside her, stroking mercilessly, magnificently, while the dancers whirled and the candlelight shimmered until she surrendered to the wicked pleasure with a violent shudder and bucked wildly against him, swept beyond propriety by the hot flood of her orgasm. Her head thrashed; the delicate ribbons of her harlequin mask snapped. It fell unheeded into the hungry, flickering flames of the candelabra below."

Lacey paused dramatically, breathlessly, her shiny red lips parted and her lashes half-lowered. "Well," she said sweetly after a moment of utter silence, "I believe I'll just stop right there and let y'all enjoy the rest of the story on your own."

Jericho released a huge breath. Amalie slumped in her chair. With scrupulous care, they did *not* look at each other.

LIL WINGO WATCHED bleary-eyed from the front seat of the limo as Madame X cuddled with Lars Torberg, who touted himself as the Nordic Arnold Schwarzenegger. When they tapped champagne glasses, she desultorily raised her camera and clicked off a few frames, then slumped down on the seat, rolling her eyes at the uniformed chauffeur. "You got anything to eat?"

Rosie Bass had begged off after dinner, so the glamorous blond lovebirds were bookended by Madame X's publicist and agent. To keep out of camera range, Amalie had been forced to share the jump seat with Jericho. She wiggled, trying to pull down the narrow skirt of her melon-colored evening ensemble. What had seemed chic on Belle Isle looked small-town unsophisticated here in Manhattan. Lacey was soignée in a black velvet sheath with clinging illusion sleeves.

"Would you be more comfortable sitting on my lap?" Jericho's breath stirred the wisps of Amalie's short, dark hair and played across her ear with a shivery arousal. "I'm sure I wouldn't mind."

"I would." Worriedly, she nibbled on her lower lip. Jericho still hadn't changed his clothes and he still smelled like lime and leather...with an intoxicating hint of musky male thrown into the mix just to confound her female sensibilities. His jaw was shadowed by the prickles of his beard. At least, she assumed it was prickly. She hadn't actually touched it. She'd only imagined touching it. With the smooth back of her hand, with her fingertips, stroking gently, and with her lips, swollen and moist and eager.

Put Jericho in the appropriate costume—killer sunglasses, tight leather pants and maybe a long skinny velvet scarf wrapped around his neck, drooping across his gleaming bare chest, give them both other identities—he was a rock star leaving in a limo after a sold-out concert at Madison Square Garden and she was a groupie who'd do *anything* for his approval—and, voilà, she had another story idea.

Stop it, she commanded herself. *Please, please, stop it.* Her imagination had been on a rampage ever since Lacey's stunning reading of "Black Velvet Mardi Gras" earlier in the evening. As Amalie saw it, her only cure was getting as far away from Jericho as she could, which by the looks of it was not going to happen.

He wasn't helping the situation by putting his arm around her shoulders. When she tried to slide away, he said, "I'm just getting comfortable, Emily," and palmed her shoulder, urging her to sink back against the soft leather seat. "Relax, Emily."

Amazingly, she did. She sank into a cocoon of his scent and his hard body beside her and his crooning voice whispering her name—

She bolted upright. "Did you say—" Had he actually called her *Amalie?*

"Isn't Emily your real name?" Jericho asked, all innocence. "Then it must be Madame X's. Emily what, I wonder?"

"It's not! I swear it's not either of our names!"

Slouched in the jump seat, he looked deceptively unconcerned. "You're fibbing."

She was, but not about this. "I swear my name is not Emily." Her hands clenched into fists in her lap. "Madame X's name is not Emily."

"No?" Jericho glanced at Madame X, who was holding up her fluted glass as Lars refilled it with champagne. The actor was smitten; although after the reading he'd invited them to go club hopping around Manhattan as a group, clearly he had eyes only for the celebrity author.

"Where did you hear it?" Amalie demanded. Jericho had come too close to the truth for her comfort. She was hoping he wouldn't realize it.

"From Norris Yount, last night," he admitted. "I overheard him calling one of you Emily just before Rosie and I came into the office."

Amalie shook her head. "You must have heard wrong."

He shrugged. "I'll check into it."

"How will you do that?"

He placed his splayed fingers on her midriff and gently shoved until she was again tucked beneath the shelter of his outstretched arm. "I have my ways."

That was what Amalie was afraid of.

"Yo, Emily," Jericho said suddenly, his voice loud in the leather-and-burled-walnut interior of the limousine.

Lacey jerked to attention as if she'd been zapped with a live wire, covering Amalie's own involuntary response to her near name. "Amalie?" Lacey blurted in confusion, her gaze skipping between them as she tried to figure out what was going on. "Did you tell—"

"He said Emily," Amalie interrupted. "*Emily.*"

After a beat, Lacey resorted to her Marilyn, but even the practiced smile was strained. "Try again, Jericho, darlin'. I only answer to Madame X."

"How about just X?" Lars said, cupping her jaw in his massive hand and turning her face back to his.

Lacey nuzzled his cheek. "For you, darlin'…" She began cooing sweet nothings in his ear.

"Interesting," Jericho purred, settling back in the seat with a satisfied sound.

"You haven't proved a thing."

"No, but now I have some ideas of where to look."

Amalie glared at him, hoping that he was bluffing. *A Hundred and One Sneaky Reporter Tricks.*

"Don't be mad."

"I'm going to ask Rosie to revoke your privileges. Madame X doesn't need a conspiracy nut like you profiling her in a national magazine." Out of the corner of her eye, Amalie saw that her agent, one of the keepers of Madame X's secret identity, looked worried. Fortunately, the publicist from Pebblepond Press was too dazzled by Lars Torberg to question Amalie's byplay with Jericho.

His face was near enough for her to discern the inner core of steel that belied the lazy sensuality of his long lashes and the pale green irises that she'd seen up close were also glazed with a hint of gold. "Freedom of the press isn't a privilege, Lacey," he said. "It's a right."

Even though she knew it was hopeless, even though she knew he was nothing but trouble, Amalie was struck with the desire to hear Jericho speak her name, her real name. She wanted to have him murmur it in her ear on a dance floor and shout it across the windswept dunes and moan it with a soul-searing passion in the blackest depths of the night. She, the demure creator of other women's fantasies, finally wanted a real one of her own. No matter how hard she tried to deny it, how fervently she blocked him from her consciousness, the truth of it kept slipping back into her mind, demanding her acknowledgment. She wanted Thomas Janes Jericho.

And she could never have him. Never.

A COUPLE OF HOURS LATER, the publicist and agent had gone home. Lil Wingo had gotten her second wind when they'd arrived at the third club of the night, and she'd had the good luck to snap a photo of a superhot sitcom hunk in lip lock with a society babe whose mogul husband was off doing a business deal in Singapore. Lil was presently circling the crowded dance floor, waiting for Madame X and Lars Torberg to maneuver into the perfect dirty-dancing pose.

Amalie was wilting. And she still couldn't elude Jericho.

He was shouting at her over the din of the music. "Do you want a drink?"

Too dizzy to manage a shake of her head, she mouthed, "No, thanks." The club was as hot as a steambath. Her eyeballs felt poached in their sockets. It was exhausting to stay on constant guard so she could keep out of the way of Lil's camera lens. Amalie wanted a drink, but she couldn't handle anything alcoholic. Jericho kept asking. Although she suspected a nefarious motive, it wasn't the usual one. The only reason he wanted her tipsy was to see what she'd reveal about Madame X. Darn it.

"So how long have you worked for Madame X?" he yelled.

She cupped her hand over her ear, pretending she hadn't understood him.

He tried again. "Is it a full-time job?"

"A fur-lined tub?" she shouted. The effort made her head swim. She put her glasses in her purse and rubbed her eyes.

Jericho gave her a long look, then grabbed her hand and pulled her out of the weaving, costumed throng that rimmed the dance floor. The decibel level lowered a notch. "I'm taking you back to the hotel," he said, and she was too grateful to fake a misunderstanding. He motioned his intentions to Lil, who would relay a message to Madame X.

It was cold outside. The kids standing in line were shivering in their combat boots and rhinestone heels and lug-soled sneakers. Amalie looked down at her own basic pumps. "Don't you have to stick with Madame X?" she asked, lifting her face to the brisk night air. The black wisps and spikes of her perspiration-soaked hair began to stiffen.

Jericho hailed a taxicab. "Nope. I've seen enough for tonight."

"She and Lars might sneak off together—without you." Amalie climbed into the cab. "You could lose a big story."

He slid in beside her. "I've got a better story right here."

She was afraid to ask what he meant. "I can find my own way back to the hotel."

"Now that wouldn't be gentlemanly of me, would it, Miss Emily?" he drawled.

She snapped out the address of her hotel to the driver. The cab lurched away from the curb. "Please don't call me that. Emily is not my name. I don't—" She gritted her teeth. "I did not lie to you."

"About that, maybe not."

"Are all journalists so suspicious?"

Jericho's mouth thinned. "The good ones. It's why they ask so many questions. It's why they uncover corruption, deception and scandal."

"And also why they ruin the lives of innocent people."

Jericho took her jaw in his hand to turn her face toward his. "I'll make you a promise, *darlin'*." His eyes were hard but mesmerizing; Amalie couldn't look away. His fingertips drifted upward to brush over the sensitive curve of her ear before coming to rest on her shoulder. "If you're innocent, you have nothing to worry about from me."

She shrugged beneath his hand. Most likely he knew that she wouldn't be comforted by such a promise, since she was as guilty as all get-out. Her lower lip quivered; she caught it between her teeth. Jericho's gold-tipped lashes dipped minutely and she knew he was looking at her mouth, just as he had been when she'd finally glanced at him a full five minutes after Lacey's dramatic reading had ended. It took all Amalie's willpower not to lick her lips. *Or his,* she admitted to herself, profoundly appalled that, despite Jericho's intentions to destroy her life, she was still fantasizing herself into compromising situations with him.

Situations like an elegant blond man in the back seat of a cab wearing a tuxedo with black velvet lapels, and the driver, her short black curls tucked up under a slouch cap, and how their steamy gazes would meet in the mirror and she'd pull the cab into a deserted alley and get into the back seat, looking straight into his sea green eyes when she said…she said—

The fantasy flew out of Amalie's head the instant Jericho kissed her. For once, reality was better than imagination.

His bottom lip touched hers. She felt the heat of his breath, then the slick, soft tip of his tongue as it slid along the seam of her lips and touched one corner of her mouth. Reflexively, her own tongue unfurled to meet his. Tingling all over, aroused and yet alarmed, she melted into his arms. Her lips parted as a full-bodied, sighing moan slipped free.

It was a helpless, heedless, honeyed sound—the sound of her surrender. The very last thing she could allow.

4

He'd been waist deep in the ocean when he saw her hit the beach, running as freely as a child on holiday, her dark hair a velvet flag in the wind. Her full breasts moved beneath the nightgown, unrestricted, enticing, and a thick heat filled his groin despite the sting of the cold water.

Not a child. A woman. A lush, lovely woman, the barely obscured shadow between her rounded thighs beckoning him with promises of a darkly sweet midnight gift.

She wanted to run from his approach. He couldn't blame her; he was engorged, body and soul, with an unrelenting need that would have scared away even the boldest of women.

Yet she stayed. Perhaps because her need matched his own: immediate, consuming, undeniable.

Beyond all convention.

JERICHO FELT her resistance melt. Felt the vulnerable feminine surrender of it hit him with a wallop, deep in the viscera of his unexpectedly strong desire. He groaned with his own kind of surrender and gathered her up, his hands slipping down to her bottom as he pulled her into his lap, his urgency making him hold her tighter than he ought to.

He ate hungry kisses from her gasping lips, greedy

kisses, his hands stroking up her narrow back. Suddenly he wanted to devour her. He wanted to strip her naked and part her innocent thighs and plunge inside her, emptying his heart and soul and endless passion into the welcoming home of her soft womanly body.

Nothing amusing in that, he dimly acknowledged, although the disturbing thought was not enough to stay his hunger. Not when she whimpered and pressed her palms to his chest, her tongue again darting tentatively toward his. He coaxingly stroked one fingertip over the swell of her bottom lip, his tongue dipping inside to meet hers, luring it to venture deeper. She tasted clean and pure, yet their kisses were blatantly erotic.

Even in the midst of such excess, Jericho's reasoning sharpened. The shy assistant was perhaps not so shy; she was certainly more than the amusing dalliance he'd expected. Which, considering his objective, might play to his short-term advantage, but would ultimately cause more complications than he wanted to deal with.

So. He raked his fingers through her tousled black hair and nuzzled her neck, muttering into it, "One hell of a road trip," knowing that the words would make her pull away. His left arm tightened around her waist despite his intentions. Raging hormones demanded a more satisfying outlet.

The assistant's chin lifted. "Pardon?" Her eyes were hazy, steeped with sexual arousal; her lips were a plump rosy pink.

Jericho grinned even though he'd rarely felt less like grinning. He patted her cheek, his fingers aching to turn the dismissive gesture into a caress. "I said I'm looking forward to one hell of a road trip."

Coloring, she looked down at her hands, splayed across his chest. "That's what I thought you said." Her tone was prickly. She made fists against his leather jacket and for an instant he was certain that she was going to hit him or push him or at least screech an enraged oath. He would've welcomed it if she had; he needed the abrupt breakaway.

Instead she carefully extricated her body from his with an air of dainty distaste. Pressing her spine into the car seat, she tugged at her hiked-up skirt. "This was a mistake."

The cab pulled up to her hotel and she stiffly exited at once, shooting Jericho a quelling look when he moved toward her. "A mistake that will not be repeated," she said, quiet but firm. "Under any circumstances."

Jericho watched her sweep past the doorman, head high, face immobile, skirt askew. "Wanna bet?" he murmured, his warm breath clouding the streaked glass of the cab window.

The taxi driver chuckled.

BY THE NEXT AFTERNOON they were at a mall in suburban Philadelphia. It had one of those pseudo-British names like Bridgecourt or Ridgecrest, and there was an impressive number of *Black Velvet* readers lined up on the pseudocobblestones paving the walkway outside the bookstore. Madame X's table was positioned at the front of the store, beside what had been an extravagant head-high pyramid display of her newest release until the customers had descended and carried the books off like victorious hunters, brandishing the freshly purchased and autographed spoils with squeals of glee.

Madame X—whoever she was, Jericho thought—was a pro. Dressed in white topped by a pearl-trimmed, black velvet vest, she had a charming word or two for each reader in line, happily scrawling her unique signature as the assistant remained silent but alert at her side. Goldilocks seemed to be enjoying her moment in the limelight.

Jericho couldn't say the same for the dark-haired assistant. He'd been watching Lacey—if that was her name—even more closely than the attention-grabbing author. Her expression was strained. He couldn't say that it was because of the stress of the book-signing event, however. She'd looked just as uptight and on guard when they'd all boarded a shuttle flight out of New York that morning. She'd flinched noticeably when she and Jericho had reached for the same piece of luggage, so it wasn't male ego alone that made him wonder if it had been his kisses that had flustered her.

As he watched, she exchanged words with Madame X and quickly slipped away from the table to find the bookstore manager at the cash register. A moment later, her brow furrowed, she was walking out of the store, hurrying past Jericho, whom she acknowledged only by studiously ignoring him.

He put down the book he'd been leafing through and followed her.

She sped up. He brushed past the last two women in line even though they were having an interesting discussion about the effect of Madame X's fiction on their love lives. "My husband can't wait for *Black Velvet III*," one of them said with a sportive giggle, despite her severe business suit and bulging day planner.

Jericho caught up to the assistant and touched her shoulder. "What's up?"

She spun around, her posture defensive. "Honestly!"

"Yes, honestly." There was a challenge in the way he stressed the word.

"That wasn't what I meant." She blew out an irritated breath, looking past his shoulder at the pseudo-mossy fountain at the center of the mall. "Can't you leave me alone?" She gestured at the bookstore. "Aren't you supposed to be observing Madame X?"

"Curiosity got the better of me." *And instinct.*

"Fine." She started off again. "I'm only going to the food court to get Madame X a diet soda, but if accompanying me is vital to your article..." She shrugged.

"Kissing you wasn't vital, either, but I did it anyway."

She turned on him. "I'd rather you didn't mention that again." Stricken with a thought, she added warily, "I'm not going to be in this article of yours, am I?"

She did have a way of piquing his curiosity. "That's yet to be determined," he said, to measure her reaction.

"Please don't."

"Most people love publicity. And having their picture taken," he added, remembering how she carefully stayed in the background whenever Lil was round.

"I'm shy," she said desperately. "I'd prefer not to be mentioned."

She looked so worried that Jericho unwisely tried to lighten the mood. "I guess it depends on how much of an impression kissing you makes on me."

"*Made* on you," she corrected, her pale cheeks turning pink. They were both aware of the low-level current of electricity that ran beneath her careful reserve. "Past tense, remember? It's not going to happen again."

He grinned, his senses percolating in response. "That's also yet to be determined." His gaze dropped to her mouth; the way she bit her lower lip was infinitely provocative.

"I'm not your plaything," she insisted, but there was a tiny catch in her voice. She walked off, her fists clenched at her sides, then whirled around again.

"And you won't learn anything incriminating from me, so you may as well stop trying!"

"What are you hiding?" Jericho murmured to himself as he watched her go, resisting the impulse to run after her and take her in his arms so he could hear again that soft sigh of surrender. She was keeping secrets; he should want to expose her, not comfort her. He should concentrate on her identity, not the scent of her skin and the taste of her lips.

Deliberately he asked himself if it was possible that the "assistant" had written the *Black Velvet* books. And if not, why did she intrigue him more than the supposed author, the overtly sexy Madame X?

His thoughts turned relentlessly to the memory of their taxicab interlude. The rush of sensation had been stronger than any other in his experience, even though he hadn't exactly been a monk up to this point. Far from it. He enjoyed women. He'd enjoyed them on four continents and in countless countries, responsibly and on a temporary basis, of course, being in no hurry to sacrifice either his well-being or his independence.

Yet kissing the black-haired pixie had been...

At a loss, he watched her stalk away, her neat little hips twitching beneath a conservative, blue wool skirt. Kissing her had been astounding. There was no reason for it—she hadn't employed techniques from the *Kama Sutra*, and his favorite type of woman up to now had been a lush, leggy redhead. The only other option was one he didn't care to contemplate. He'd learned long ago to keep his deepest emotions disengaged from the matter at hand, so the likelihood that he'd already developed deep feelings for her was more or less impossible.

He was on a mission to expose Madame X, whomever she might turn out to be. Sentiment had no place within him.

Gauging that he had ten minutes before the assistant returned, Jericho reentered the bookstore. The line was finally dwindling.

"Congratulations, Madame X," he said, taking the empty chair beside her, "you're a real pro. Didn't Rosie tell me you've never done publicity before?"

Madame X's smile was so quick and warm it would've been easy for him to overlook that it was also practiced to a polish. "Darlin', that's my natural charm," she said coyly, and turned the smile on a gangly young man in a Temple U sweatshirt. "Do you spell that *S-E-A-N?*"

The college boy stammered out a fawning compliment while Madame X personalized his copy. With a sly wink at Jericho, she puckered her lips and made her mark on the title page. He maintained a blank expression, but inside he wondered, once again, what had become of the book the assistant had snatched away from him the previous night.

The next person in line was a plump seventy-year-old bearing a plate of brownies and copies of both books. "I loved the story where the bachelor bakes brownies in the buff," she said. "Then he opens the oven and—"

"Ouch," Jericho interjected.

Madame X nodded. "An apron would have been practical, but fortunately, in a fantasy nothing is essential."

"So he drops a hot pad in the oven and starts a fire," the woman said.

"And a beautiful firefighter rescues him," Madame X finished fondly, signing both books. "In more ways than one."

"A naked man in the kitchen is my favorite fantasy. It's like you read my mind."

"Better than a naked man needing ointment in the kitchen," Jericho muttered, trying to remain caustic though he'd conjured up his own image of a pansy-eyed pixie wearing nothing but an apron. Preferably a half apron, and the brownies would have to wait while they started the kind of fire water doesn't put out.

Confounded by his unusually overactive imagination, he slid lower in the chair, stretching out his legs. Must be the *Black Velvet* aura getting to him. Maybe the ban-Madame-Xers were right. A little erotica was a dangerous thing.

Having kicked something under the table, he lifted the black velvet cloth to see what was there. He'd toppled the assistant's lumpy leather satchel. A book and a sheaf of papers had slid out. When he reached down to retrieve them, the brush of velveteen covers under his fingertips prompted all his senses to go on alert.

Madame X was leisurely signing books for the half-dozen remaining fans. Casually Jericho leaned forward, his elbows on his knees. He glanced at Madame X and then away, hanging his head to unobtrusively peruse the copy of *Black Velvet II.* No guaranteeing it was the same book, but... He flipped it open. There was the red lipstick mark, his name, an inscription...no, *a telephone number.*

Instantly recognizing the Manhattan exchange, he committed the digits to memory and returned the book to its place. He was nonchalantly inching the bag farther beneath the table when the assistant reappeared with several soft drinks in tall paper cups, drinking straws poking out from between her fingers like porcupine quills. She stripped off their paper covers and punched them through the lids. "How's it going?" she asked, taking in the situation at a glance.

Jericho straightened, trying to look blameless. He wouldn't confront her until he'd checked out the phone number. "Rather well," he said blandly. "Care for a brownie?"

She confronted the plate of baked goods warily, making him think she was aware of the story they referred to. "No, thank you," she finally said, sounding as though she suspected *him* of cooking up shenanigans.

The bookstore owner bustled over to them before Jericho could comment. She enthused with Madame X over the success of the event, congratulating her on the poetic yet accessible quality of her erotica. The assistant stepped aside quietly and retrieved the leather satchel from beneath the table, quickly snapping it shut when she realized it was open. Tense and withdrawn, she clutched it to her chest, her eyes dark with what appeared to Jericho to be sadness. Or regret.

Not because of his kiss, he decided, his gaze flitting between the exuberant Madame X and her unobtrusive assistant. Unable to deny that he was drawn only to the pixie, he blamed the attraction on his piqued suspicions.

For such an observant man, Thomas Janes Jericho was on occasion willfully blind.

THE HUNT-CLUB-INSPIRED hotel lounge was dimly lit and relatively quiet, most of the cocktail crowd having gone on to dinner. Diffidently Amalie wandered inside, at loose ends now that Lacey—still portraying Madame X—had departed for a private dinner with the bookstore owner and several members of her reading group. Lacey had urged Amalie to come along for what promised to be an enjoyable evening of good food and literary talk, but Amalie hadn't seen the point. After a long day of guarding Madame X against mistakes and Jericho's intrusions, she craved quiet and solitude. Since Jericho, her main worry, wasn't following Lacey to the dinner, Amalie felt safe in trusting her friend to carry on the Madame X impersonation without a chaperon.

Amalie bypassed the tables and sank into one of the burgundy leather wing chairs that flanked the fireplace. While she hadn't counted on the stress of constantly defending herself from Jericho—and others, of course, though her mind seemed stuck mainly on the treacherous journalist—what she found even more disturbing was the usurping of her rightful role as Madame X. Sanctioned though it was.

She didn't blame Lacey. After all, Lacey was only doing what had been asked of her, and doing it so well that even Amalie was half believing the charade. As she hadn't wanted to take on the role herself, by all rights she should've been overjoyed that Lacey was managing so well.

A waitress arrived. Amalie asked for a glass of wine instead of her usual soft drink. The alcohol might help her relax. She needed to stop fretting over the apparent success of her lies.

The heat of the fire enveloped her, easing her mind as its warmth seeped into her bones. Amalie's gaze drifted from the orange flames to the brick surround and the carved wood mantel arranged with slightly tarnished trophies and black-and-white photos of top-hatted men on purebred hunters and veiled women jumping sidesaddle. It was easy to imagine away the hotel lounge as long as she kept her back to the clusters of candlelit cocktail tables and focused on the fire, on the mesmerizing patterns of flickering light and shadow it threw across the hearth.

She could have been an equestrian, sprawled before the fireplace after a morning's hunt through the crisp November countryside, bone weary and still redolent of horses and leather and the outdoors, her black velvet helmet resting on her knee and her mud-spattered stock untied. Amalie smiled to herself and shifted pleasurably.

Then the master of the hunt might come in, tall and handsome in his red jacket with black velvet lapels, his haughty face ruddy with cold. She'd lift her leg desultorily and have the audacity to ask him, a respected, wealthy landowner whose daughter had been her finishing school classmate, to help her off with her boots. He might look coldly at her with his pale green eyes and she'd return the stare, her lips curving as she lazily stroked one hand down her shirtfront, slowly rubbing her thighs together until his eyes were no longer icy but simmering with lust. He'd turn his back on her and bend over in his skintight jodhpurs, taking her booted foot insinuatingly between his heavily muscled thighs so he could tug—

"Here you go," said the waitress, presenting a goblet of red wine. "Will there be anything else?"

"No, no, thank you," Amalie responded after a beat, squirming out of her slumped position in the leather chair so she could take the glass. "Thank you very much," she said again, flustered, agitated, much too aware of the heat flushing her cheeks and quickening her blood.

Amalie fanned herself. The only way she could dismiss the persistent fantasy—the hunt master would sink to his knees and whisper hot metaphors about mounting and riding as he skinned off her jodhpurs—

was by returning to her previous thoughts. Better to worry over what was wrong with her than what was right with Jeri—the master of the hunt. Why wasn't she satisfied when everything, save one pesky reporter, was working out as planned?

She'd never thought of herself as a jealous person. Nor an egotist. Still, even though she hadn't wanted the notoriety of Madame X, now that she wasn't getting any of the acclaim, either, she couldn't help but feel left out. It was irrational, but there it was.

And it was no one's fault but her own.

She'd gotten exactly what she'd schemed for.

Too late to regret it now, she scolded herself, even though that was exactly what she was doing, the images of naked, sweaty bodies tangled on the rug before the fireplace pushed far to the back of her mind. She hoped.

JERICHO FOUND HER tucked deep in a massive wing chair, looking frail in her oversize, pink knitted sweater over skinny black leggings, one leg curled beneath the other. She stared broodingly into the fire as she nursed a glass of wine, her face more open and vulnerable without her glasses. The sight of her, rosy cheeked and sleepy, deep in thoughts that he'd give anything to read, made a crackling excitement flare within him. It was similar to and yet conspicuously different from the zeal he felt when he was going for the kill on a big story. The inconstancy made him hesitate before he approached. Did he want to defraud her or make love to her?

He'd tried the mysterious phone number at the first opportunity. An answering machine had picked up, one with a message that was as frustrating as it was inconclusive. A woman with a lilting Southern voice had not identified herself, but merely confirmed the number dialed and asked the caller to leave the customary message after the beep. His first instinct was that the voice did in fact belong to Madame X, but as she and her assistant sounded so similar, he couldn't be certain. Even if the voice belonged to the assistant, he'd proved nothing, since she could've easily taped her employer's message.

At any rate, the question of identities would be solved once he got his hands on a reverse telephone directory, where he could look up the number first and match it to a name. Best-case scenario, he'd have uncovered Madame X's real identity—or the imposter's—within twenty-four hours.

Maybe worst-case scenario, he admitted with some regret, looking at the cameo-style purity of the assistant's drooping profile. Although he might like to draw out their time together, playing a cat-and-mouse game with her and Madame X didn't particularly appeal. He preferred a straight-ahead, face-to-face confrontation, with no tricky feints or manipulations. Even when he hadn't been accorded the same courtesy.

Too bad such an approach would murder his chances with his velvet-haired, sad-eyed, sweet-tasting mystery lady.

He hovered behind her for another moment, then put his hands on the back of her chair and leaned down to speak softly over her shoulder. "You look lonely."

She started, wine sloshing in the bottom of her goblet, but recovered quickly. "I'm alone, not lonely. I *like* being alone," she said smartly, steadying the glass on her knee as she shrank back against the padded leather.

He was purposely obtuse. "Then you don't mind if I join you."

Amalie couldn't help but laugh, her midnight blue eyes gleaming in the light of the fire as she watched him settle into the other chair. "Do you know the poem about the fog stealing in on little cat's paws?" she asked on impulse. "I'm going to write a Thomas Jericho version. 'The yellow journalist steals in on sneaky cougar's paws....'"

He crossed one denim-clad leg over the other and tapped the sole of his leather boots, as if to disprove his culpability. "Which part should I object to first—yellow or sneaky?"

"You *are* always sneaking up on me."

"You're so aloof, that's the only way I dare to approach you."

She frowned. "I'm aloof?"

He smiled. "But that doesn't put me off."

"More's the pity," she drawled, sticking her nose up in the air.

"Honey, you don't fool me," he said easily. "You're more shy than snooty. And even though you might normally like to be alone, tonight you're feeling lonely."

"I suppose that's true," Amalie found herself admitting, possibly because she was disarmed by the word *honey.* He hadn't really meant it, she decided. It had been only a casual turn of phrase, and now she'd left herself exposed. "Um, I mean that I miss my hometown, is all."

"Where's that?"

She hesitated, but couldn't come up with a good reason not to answer, at least in generalities. "An island off the South Carolina coast."

"Like Hilton Head?"

"Not so ritzy," she said, which was true even though it was also true that the Dove family owned approximately half of Belle Isle's three square miles. "And no-where near as developed. On a map, we're a tiny little dot of no particular notice."

"Must be a nice place."

Was he prying? Or just being friendly? Maybe she really was homesick, because she opted to believe the latter. "The air is so sweet this time of the year. Soon the honeysuckle and magnolia will be in bloom."

"Do you get back to visit very often?"

"Back?" she blurted.

"I was assuming you live near Madame X. In Manhattan, was it?"

"Oh, yes, you're right, of course. But, no, we don't necessarily live in Manhattan." Amalie was uncomfortable with lying to him. Nor could she fathom his assumption about Manhattan when he knew they'd been staying at a hotel. "Madame X chooses not to reveal her residence, you see. And I—I still think of the island as home."

Jericho nodded. "Yes, I see."

Amalie tried to think straight. She had to maintain her suspicions about his motives no matter how friendly—or seductive—he appeared. "Please tell me that every word out of my mouth isn't going to appear in print."

For a moment Jericho seemed contemplative, but then his expression eased into the practiced charm he'd used before to disarm her. "Don't you recognize polite conversation when you hear it?"

"How do I know this isn't number sixty-two of *A Hundred and One Sneaky Reporter*—"

"I'm starting to resent that word."

"*Sneaky?* I can't imagine why."

His eyebrows arched. "There may be a sneak present, but I can promise you it isn't me."

Amalie looked down at the inch of wine remaining in her goblet. Her fingertips pressed hard against the ridges of the thick cut-glass stem. "Our polite conversation seems to be deteriorating."

"That happens to us pretty often, doesn't it?" Jericho observed. He lapsed into silence again, then moved restlessly, crossing and recrossing his legs, running his thumb along the whitened seam of his jeans. "Sorry."

She exhaled. "I'm sorry, too."

"We can go off the record, if you'd prefer."

While that was better, she knew she'd feel wary around him nonetheless. Which was because of his profession, she was sure, even though snapshots of her earlier fantasy were flicking past her mind's eye and Jericho looked magnificent in jodhpurs and tall black boots...and nothing else. She cleared her throat. "Going off the record only works if I can believe you'll honor your word. I don't—"

"Careful," he warned. "I suspect you're on the verge of calling me sneaky again." He leaned forward, his eyes like a mint julep—frosty but refreshing. "I'm a straight shooter...Lacey. No two ways about it. If I say you're off the record, you can bank on it."

She caught the hesitation before her fake name. And the implication. Jericho might be a straight shooter, but he was also relentless. She could darn well rock-solid bank on his digging until he uncovered the truth about her and Madame X.

There was no hope of him abandoning the story, so in order to protect her quiet life on Belle Isle she must resolve to communicate with him as little as possible for the length of the book tour.

"Have you had dinner?" he asked, not privy to her decision. "Would you like to try the hotel dining room?"

Amalie intended to put him off, but what came out when she opened her mouth was a noncommittal murmur. "Mmm, I'm too lazy to move away from this wonderful fire."

Before she knew it Jericho was calling the waitress over and asking for sandwiches to be served in front of the fireplace. With a bottle of wine, he suggested, looking to Amalie for her approval. She slid her feet to the floor, intending to protest. He overrode her, requesting something delicious and full of calories for dessert, seeing as how his impromptu dinner date was on the *Black Velvet* diet.

She rolled her bottom lip between her teeth, fighting the desire to succumb. Jericho was being too nice. She shouldn't be taken in by the charm he seemed to turn on and off at will.

Still, the possibilities of their coming together zipped through her faster than she could stop them. It would be hazardous, but so tempting. Oh, if only once she dared to break her bonds of modesty and restraint!

Accustomed to caution, Amalie leaned back, sinking into the depths of the wing chair and tucking her chin into the thick layers of her sweater's turtleneck. She *was* a turtle, pulling in when danger approached, hoping to survive the tumult right side up, with her shell intact. Pitiful, she thought. Just about what one would expect of a shy librarian-curator-archivist from an island backwater, a woman too timid to own up to her own fantasies. She really had to do something about her Milquetoast tendencies.

Someday. Someday soon.

5

"No names," Amy Lee agreed with a whisper. Her voice jittered; her chin quivered. She couldn't help herself. She was trembling inside and out, vibrantly out of control.

Nervously she plucked at her damp gown, lifting it out of the water, bunching it in wet folds that clung to her trembling legs. The stranger's eyes were like coals; his hot gaze burned her skin. She pressed her fist between her breasts, drawing the thin cotton tight across her prominent nipples. Her heart thumped wildly, ready to burst through her chest in its explosive desire.

Her fantasy man brushed his fingertips across her knuckles. As if there was magic in his touch, her fist automatically turned and loosened, offering him her palm, the fragile inside of her wrist. His head bowed over it and his lips moved against her damp palm, his tongue seeking the racing pulse below.

Amy Lee almost swooned. She was a demure schoolteacher—she could not do this! "I can't," she breathed. "I shouldn't."

He put his hand across her mouth. "Hush."

"DOVECOTE?" Jericho said. "Your tree house had a name?"

Amalie crunched down hard on a dill pickle, its tang

making her lips pucker. Although the name had slipped out, there was no reason to think he could make anything of it. "Sort of," she mumbled. "Unofficially." The name Dovecote was carved into the lintel of the tree house, a structure so elaborate it was a perfect miniature of the Southern Gothic family home.

She'd been telling him about her childhood gang on Belle Isle, how they'd played pirate on the beach, exploring an ancient shipwreck that was nothing but a pile of rotted beams uncovered by the shifting dunes, "sailing" a rowboat through the salt marshes, making maps that led to buried shoe box treasure chests full of gold-spray-painted rocks. Dovecote was the fancy tree house a Dove ancestor had built in one of the grand old live oaks that grew near the family home. It had been the center of her childhood adventures until Amalie turned thirteen and moved with her parents to Washington, D.C., to attend a swank prep school. She'd returned a year later for summer vacation, so tamed, polished and well behaved that her island friends were uncomfortable with her. They'd begun treating her differently, and after that, nothing had been the same.

"Marydoe, the housekeeper, would make us box lunches," she remembered aloud, "and we'd stay outside until she rang the evening bells to call us home. Sometimes we convinced our parents to let us spend the night in the tree house, but then one of us—usually me—would see Blackbeard's ghost prowling the beach and we'd run shrieking through the woods until we reached the lights of Southsea Road."

She chewed the last bite of a roast beef on pumpernickel sandwich, gazing fondly at the fire, aware at the back of her mind that Jericho was watching her closely. "Ruby, Moses, Charlie and me. We were a gang of four."

"So which one grew up to become Madame X?" Jericho asked casually, by all appearances more interested in scooping up coleslaw than hearing her answer.

Since *she* had grown up to be Madame X, the question was loaded. Still, Amalie felt comfortable enough to treat it like a joke. "Who says any of them did?" she countered sassily, rolling her eyes at Jericho.

"You and Madame X have the same accent, so naturally I wondered."

"It just so happens that we both grew up in small South Carolina towns. I didn't meet—" Amalie almost said *Lacey* "—Madame X until college." She put her mustard-daubed plate back on the small round table between their chairs and observed the wreckage of their dinner order. There was only an inch of wine left in the bottle. "Did I really eat all this?"

The waitress swept in, removed their used dishes and returned with thick slices of a dark chocolate cake. "The dessert chef's specialty," she said. "He calls it black velvet layer cake."

Slack jawed, Amalie pointed her finger at Jericho. "You can't be serious."

He pointed back at her tauntingly, then flicked his fingertip across the gooey chocolate frosting and brought it up to his lips. "Mmm. I saw the cake on the menu earlier and I knew we had to try it."

"It looks wonderful, but I'm full enough to burst."

He forked up a generous portion and offered it to her. "Just one bite."

Amalie was tempted. However, having used the food-as-seduction ploy in one of her short stories, she knew what was afoot. Just the same, she might've succumbed if she'd been sure that Jericho was after her and not inside information on Madame X.

She picked up her own fork and tasted the cake. "Delicious."

He looked disappointed, but ate the bite he'd intended for her and then licked the tines provocatively. "So..." he murmured, his voice so low it seemed to vibrate in the marrow of her bones.

Amalie said nothing. This was the moment toward the end of the evening when a man's intentions became clear. Would Jericho ask her up to his room? Eagerly accompany her to her own? Would he at the very least kiss her, with that magnificent skill she'd been aching to experience again despite her stiff-necked denials? Her stomach rolled in anticipation.

He put down his fork and slid the table back several inches so he could lean closer to her. The fire crackled and popped; other noises from the half-filled lounge seemed to dim.

"So, Lacey, what happened to the other members of the gang of four?"

Amalie blinked. He was still asking his own questions, not answering hers. And although he'd listened to her ramblings, seeming to be genuinely interested, the brutal truth was that his interest probably extended only as far as she related to Madame X. Amalie tugged at the collar of her sweater, trying not to feel bereft now that Jericho's intentions were clear.

She gave him a nonchalant shrug. "Moses was our housekeeper's oldest son. He worked his way through college and became a lawyer. He lives in Charleston. I see him now and then when he visits Marydoe." She shot Jericho an appraising look, wondering if he really cared about her childhood buddies, even one who'd done some confidential legal work concerning her pseudonym and copyright. Or was he still hoping she'd slip and reveal Madame X?

"Ruby was the rebel," she continued. "Her family situation was rather unfortunate, and she resented being labeled poor white trash by some of the islanders. She married early, then divorced. I didn't hear from her for years, but now she's back on the island, waitressing at our only year-round restaurant. And Charlie skipped from job to job for a while before he settled in as the manager of the airport. He has a wife and two kids." Amalie stood, twining her arms together like a nervous schoolgirl as she looked down on Jericho. "None of my childhood friends write erotica in their spare time, if that's what you really wanted to know."

The firelight painted his hair with a shifting honeycomb of highlights as he rose. Amalie's insides quivered. She set her mouth primly in response, her hands clasped tightly over her breastbone. "And what about you?" he asked, stepping too close.

"You mean, what do I do in my spare time?"

"For a start."

"You go first," she insisted. "I've been answering your questions all evening—" and was surprised that she'd enjoyed it in the moments she'd forgotten to stay on guard "—so I think it's your turn."

He gave a short laugh. "All right. I'm a C-SPAN junkie. And on occasion, I rock climb, freestyle."

Immediately she pictured him clinging to the face of a steep rock, his thighs bulging, every taut muscle quivering with exertion. She was certain that his face would reveal nothing but calm control. "Freestyle means dangerous, doesn't it?" she asked. "No backup or safety harness? Aren't you afraid of falling, of—of *dying*?"

The expression in Jericho's eyes was as unyielding as the most treacherous rock he'd ever climbed. "No," he said simply.

He stood inches away, mimicking her pose with his arms crossed over his torso. She stared a tad too long at the raised veins on the back of his hands and the obvious strength of his lightly furred forearms beneath rolled-up sleeves. "You're one cool customer, huh?" she said, jerking her gaze away, trying to focus on anything but the amazing fact that such manly hands had held her so fiercely and yet gently, had stroked her so lovingly. Didn't that connote some amount of feeling for her?

She was savvy enough to know that sex didn't necessarily equate with love. Unfortunately, that didn't carry a lot of weight when her fantasies were growing beyond their bounds and Jericho was the first man she'd been really attracted to—*fatally* attracted to—in ages. Even if he was after her only for information.

"Your turn," he said.

She made herself back away. If he thought she was going to talk about her hobbies—! "Another time."

He dropped money on the table and followed her across the cocktail lounge. The round oak tables were lit now by brass-and-burgundy candlestick lamps, and her gaze jumped from table to table as she caught snatches of conversation and laughter. Couples were everywhere. A woman wearing red lipstick kissed a man in a suede jacket. Two lovers shared a whispered conversation, their foreheads almost touching. A pair who looked as if they'd been together fifty years held hands across the table. Amalie closed her eyes and barreled through the swinging doors to the corridor. Jericho caught her elbow and steered her toward the lobby.

"What did you do before Madame X hired you?" he asked, maddeningly persistent. And apparently oblivious to her mood.

They entered the elevator. "I work..." Amalie paused, concentrating on drawing a deep breath. Her lungs felt shallow, her throat tight. To say nothing of the state of her mind. She knew she couldn't blame that entirely on the stress of maintaining her lies about Madame X. "I ran the island's combination museum-archives-library. It's mainly open during the summer, so I'll probably go back to it once the *Black Velvet* tour is finished."

"Doesn't Madame X plan to write another sequel?"

The elevator doors pinged. "You'll have to ask her that," Amalie said, tired now that Jericho's intentions had been made crystal clear. He didn't want to know *her*, he wanted to know Madame X. Distractedly she ticked off door numbers as they walked along the hallway, trying to keep her mind away from itchily persistent images of Jericho's nude body bathed in firelight. "This was all off the record, correct?"

"Correct."

She paused before room 418, telling herself that fantasies were just fantasies. In her experience, they had no basis in reality. "Then good night, Jericho."

He was very still. "Good night, Lacey."

Amalie's fingers clenched around the key card she'd slipped from her pocket. The very last name she wanted him to call her was Lacey. Madame X would be more disastrous, but somehow not so heart wrenching.

Gently Jericho took the card and ran it through the slot to open her door. She let her head tip back against the door frame, knowing she should go inside but staying anyway, watching Jericho through her lowered lashes, willing him to kiss her.

He gave her a long, serious look and nudged open the door. After delaying another moment, Amalie stepped into the dark room. She'd never felt less like retiring to a solitary night filled only with erotic dreams, but Jericho was giving her no other choice.

"See you," he said, and closed the door in her face.

She slumped against the frame, more than her body aching with unresolved emotion and frustration. Her very heart felt bruised.

JERICHO STAYED in the hallway outside room 418 a long while, turning the key card in his hand. He hadn't intended to keep it, but now that it was in his possession the temptation to use it was fierce.

The question was, did he use it for good—invading "Lacey's" room to sweep her into a passionate embrace that would overwhelm both their objections? Or did he use it for evil—waiting until the assistant was asleep and slipping inside to find evidence of Madame X's real identity?

"Sneaky reporter tricks," he muttered, knowing he couldn't do the latter when it went against every one of his principles. There were better ways to come by the facts, ways he wouldn't be ashamed to admit to in print.

As for the other, though…at the very least, it would give him a semilegitimate entrée into her room.

He knocked.

She answered immediately, almost as if she'd been waiting for him. Looking at her, he hoped she had. Her heart-shaped face was solemn beneath the feathery disarray of her pixie haircut. Her eyes were wide, a deep indigo blue that beckoned to something unidentified in him, something that told him he could not take advantage of her, nor of their growing attraction. That, too, had been a foolish, weak-willed, soft-hearted option.

He extended the key card. "You forgot this."

She started to take it, then clasped his hand between both of hers and drew him closer. "Don't you want to kiss me?"

"You said—"

"Never mind what I said."

Lightly he traced his fingertips across her cheek. "I want so much to kiss you that I can't."

Her lips parted. "I know." She gave a little sigh and leaned her head against his shoulder.

He touched his lips to her hair. She smelled sweet and fresh and wild, like a tangle of beach roses in the sunshine. Were there beach roses on her island? Suddenly he wanted to see it almost as much as he wanted to take her to East Hampton and show her the rare remote hideaways he'd once searched out among the upwardly mobile crowds that crawled the countryside and beachfront.

Her eyes were closed when she turned her face up to his. "Kiss me anyway," she whispered, so shy about the request she couldn't look at him.

He wanted to see her eyes. "Look at me first."

Her lids slowly lifted, revealing expressive eyes filled with uncertainty and longing. There was the slightest hint of playfulness, too, and definitely the promise of passion.

Jericho read the overlying vulnerability in her gaze and knew he had to contain his base impulses. If this woman was the author of three books of erotica, they were the result of a naughty, overactive imagination, not worldly experience. Though she might be an imposter, she was also an innocent.

A most bewitching and quite willing innocent.

His mouth came down gently on hers, making their kiss tantalizing in its delicacy. Other needs were carefully withheld as he allowed himself only the lightest touch of his hand to her cheek, his palm under her sweater caressing the satiny skin below her rib cage. She was soft and sleek. Languid warmth simmered between them.

He withdrew slowly. She seemed lost, suspended in the moment of their kiss, her eyes closed again as she waited for his lips to descend....

"Breathe," he said, and she did with a gasp, her lashes flying up in surprise. Her laugh was husky, her eyes beseeching. He had to get rid of her.

Jericho pressed his fingertips against her midriff, careful to avoid excessive contact. "Go inside now," he directed, propelling her backward into the hotel room despite her murmured sounds of protest. He closed the door in her face for the second time, only then finishing his sentence. "Before I change my mind."

His frustration was acute. He might have battered down the door to get to her if he hadn't been so accustomed to suppressing his feelings. He walked away instead, tight and controlled, but painfully aware that he could not hold this attraction inside forever.

The dalliance was not working out as planned. There was even a chance that he was on the verge of falling in love with a woman whose name he did not know, although he stubbornly refused to accept that possibility so soon.

Except, perhaps, in the long-buried depths of his heart.

THE NEXT MORNING, Jericho was gone.

"So's Lil," Lacey said when Amalie asked her about it. They'd been picked up at the hotel by an escort the publisher had employed, and were on a quick trip around the city to hit several bookstores before catching an afternoon flight to Detroit. Madame X was to appear on a regional talk show that evening, do some quick interviews and signings, then continue on to Chicago, where they'd be joined by Minette Styles of Pebblepond Press for a two-day stay chock-full of publicity opportunities. The itinerary thrilled Lacey. It made Amalie wish she'd never left Belle Isle. Initially she'd imagined a few manageably sized book signings and ten-minute newspaper interviews far from home. She wasn't prepared for such extensive coverage—and as sales continued to grow, it was only getting worse.

"Were they finished with *NewsProfile's* Madame X story?" Amalie asked. She should have been relieved at the prospect, but she couldn't bring herself to believe that Jericho would give up just like that, and without saying goodbye.

"We're not off the hook that easily," Lacey said. She was wearing another of the Madame X costumes: a red dress with the signature black velvet piece, today a short, fitted jacket. "Lil told me that she had another assignment elsewhere but she'd meet us in Chicago. The big *NewsProfile* photo shoot is being set up for Minneapolis, the day after that writers' awards dinner dance we've all been invited to."

Amalie couldn't concentrate on anything as frivolous as a dance. "What about Jericho?"

There was more than idle curiosity to the edgy question, and Lacey's female intuition picked up on it even if her friend was too closemouthed to cooperate with the juicy details. "What all did you and Jericho get up to last night?" she jibed. "You sound mighty anxious to know where he is when only a couple days ago you wanted to see him booted out of the entourage." She laughed and rocked from side to side, hugging herself. "I love that word, don't you? I always wanted to have an entourage."

Amalie smiled reluctantly. "That's why you're the perfect Madame X, and I'm not."

"Aw…" Lacey tilted her head. "Aren't you having even a smidgen of fun being in my entourage, Am? I'll grant you Jericho, for compensation."

Amalie hid a genuine smile behind her hand. Little did Lacey know that for once Jericho wasn't hers to grant. Not that he was Amalie's either—yet. "It's true, sometimes I forget to worry and then I do love meeting the *Black Velvet* readers. It's fascinating to see how they come in all sizes and classes and ages. I'd love to be able to—" She cut herself off with a sigh. No, it wasn't feasible for her to greet the readers as the author. She had to quit wishing it was.

"And Jericho?" Lacey asked archly.

Amalie tried to scowl. "He's dangerous. I have to keep my eye on him."

"That hair, those eyes, the muscles," Lacey purred. "Poor you, it's quite a hardship."

"An inspiration," Amalie admitted shyly. "There's a whole book of fantasies in him."

"Why, Amalie, I do think you're smitten!" Lacey eyed her abashed friend. "Have you ever considered using him for something more than inspiration?"

"I don't—I couldn't. I can't." Amalie laced her fingers together tightly. "I mean, think of the implications. How could I sleep with him and then lie to his face about…" She caught the eye of the interested escort in the rearview mirror. "You know what," she finished uncomfortably, with a small flutter of her fingers warning Lacey to be careful.

"I know." Lacey remembered how Amalie had been too timid to show her first erotic short story to anyone but their sorority sisters until Lacey had made a copy and entered it into the competition for the college's Howington Prize for Literature.

Even so, at heart Amalie wasn't quite as meek as she made herself out to be. The vast multitude of *Black Velvet* readers knew it, if only anonymously. After nine years as friends, Lacey knew it even better. However, she was also aware that Amalie usually needed a jump-start to get her going.

Lacey smiled to herself as she began to plot the initial jolt. "I do know," she said, to fill the lull caused by her inner machinations. "Believe me, Amalie, darlin', I know you like a book."

AFTER TWO DAYS of fruitful research, Jericho caught up to Madame X and her entourage on their second day in Chicago. In the cab from the airport, the driver was listening to a morning radio show that featured a loud-mouthed shock jock called Bob Slob and his interview with Madame X. After a few ribald comments that elicited guffaws from an apparently brain-dead sidekick, the jock introduced Madame X to the accompaniment of a sound-effects overkill: wolf whistles and howls, heavy breathing, dog barks and an oft-repeated, breathy "oo-la-la" in a feminine French accent.

Beyond sophomoric, Jericho thought, but the cabbie was chuckling between puffs of his cigar.

Bob Slob started off the interview by making lascivious comments on Madame X's figure for the "benefit of his listening audience." When this was met by the author's total silence, the dead air convinced him to quickly move on to another subject. After a few minutes of nearly innocuous chitchat about the book and the tour, he launched into the erotica-versus-pornography debate.

Madame X wasn't having any. "There's an easy way

to tell the difference, Mr. Slob," she said, her voice smooth as silk.

Now that he was listening with an educated ear, Jericho could discern between her and the assistant even on the radio. Madame X's voice was a touch fuller and deeper. There was a trained quality about it, especially when she was in professional mode. The assistant's voice was also pleasing, but not quite as rich. At times she sounded tentative and girlish, which was a comment on her personality as well as her voice.

He'd determined that the voice on the answering machine belonged to the woman he knew as Madame X.

However, his research had revealed that the Manhattan telephone number she'd inscribed in his book was listed for Lacey Longwood, which led him to wonder if they were one and the same. And if that was the case, why was the assistant claiming to be Lacey?

He'd found it easy enough to jump to the next conclusion. A few visits to New York agents and casting directors had turned up a composite of an actress named Lacey Longwood—the same beautiful blonde who purported to be Pebblepond Press's Madame X.

Jericho's triumph was bitter. They'd tried to dupe him, and he didn't like it.

Of course, there was still a chance that the actress was indeed the author. A slim chance, by any estimation. It made no sense for the assistant to call herself Lacey, unless *she* was the mysterious author—"Emily"—and not even her publisher and editor realized it. If so, the whole escapade was a tangled mess and so risky there had to be a damn good reason the two conspirators were trying to pull it off.

Through the haze of cigar smoke, Jericho stared as the cab zipped past the Bigsby & Kruthers mural of

Chicago's notable faces. He figured he'd peeled away only the first layers of the Madame X deception and would have to proceed discreetly to prevent tipping off the imposters too soon. There could be no direct confrontation until he'd gotten a firmer hold on their motives.

He slammed his hand against his thigh. *Damn it*. He didn't like delays. He wanted to sit the pair of them down and make them tell the truth. He wanted to get to the heart of the real Madame X, and if she turned out to be Little Miss Assistant, he wanted to know why duplicity tripped off her tongue as easily as her innocent kisses.

He wanted to know if everything about her was a lie.

"FCC and station regulations would prevent you from reading true pornography over the air," Madame X was telling the shock jock. "But most of my *Black Velvet* stories could potentially be broadcast because they rely more on finely drawn titillation—" *oo-la-la* "—than explicit language. There's as much lovemaking in my books as there is sex."

"Spoken like a *la-a-ady*," jeered Bob Slob.

"Thank you very much," Madame X said, poisonously polite.

He chuckled lewdly. "It wasn't a compliment."

"That's your problem," she retorted.

Bob Slob decided to ignore her intractability. "Hey, hey, whaddya freaks out there say we get down and dirty and have Madame X read some of her hot, hot, hot stuff to test the theory out!"

Madame X waited for the canned applause and wolf whistles to die down. "I don't believe that's appropriate in this time slot."

"You said it's not pornography, am I right? You don't use words like..." A high-pitched tone drowned out a string of obscenities. The dim-witted sidekick laughed himself into a fit of apoplexy.

"Explicit terms have their place, if used sparingly," Madame X said. "I personally wouldn't be so irresponsible as to use them in a joke on the radio. Or to read from a book meant for adults at a time when young people may be listening."

A wry smile crept across Jericho's face. Whoever she was, Madame X didn't take any guff. If the quieter, more demure assistant was in fact the author, she may have been smart to hire such an adept actress to portray Madame X.

Fact was, the *Black Velvet* publicity machine was rolling along impressively. Madame X was being presented as a glib model of fashion-plate perfection, every publicist's fantasy author, and the *Black Velvet* readers seemed willing to accept her on that basis. Even Harry Bass had sicced his reporter on the story because it was sexy and would sell magazines.

Jericho swore. When the scandal broke, the press would be all over the story, but chances were that he'd be the only one who really cared about the truth.

"YOU HANDLED THAT BOOR from the radio very well," he said to Madame X some hours later in the sitting room of another luxurious hotel suite. "It made me wonder if you've had previous experience dealing with the media."

She smiled and gave him another of her noncommittal answers. "Not to any great extent."

"How illuminating," Jericho griped. He was frustrated. He'd been trying to get Madame X alone ever since the tour started, and now that he'd finally succeeded she was being as careful and bland as an on-the-fence politician. The assistant—better to call her the other imposter—could walk in the door at any time and put a stop to the interview; he'd hoped to get at least one good quote out of the fake Madame X before that happened.

So he'd go at it from another angle. "Tell me about your writing. How did you start?"

Madame X posed prettily in a thinking posture, one shiny scarlet fingernail pressed to her lips. "Do you mean, where do I get my inspiration?" she said in her most sugary, modulated tones. Then, when Jericho least expected it, she broke the pose and laughed with gusto. "That's what all the other reporters have asked!"

Objectively, she was an extremely attractive woman, with enough brains and ambition to make her more than a bimbo. *Objectively?* Jericho scoffed at himself. Since when did a woman like Madame X make him think objectively, even in his capacity as a journalist?

"I was thinking more along the lines of mechanics—"

She winked. "Body mechanics?"

Jericho shook his head. "How do you plot your stories? How do you come up with the characterizations? What were your literary influences?"

She hesitated. "Well, I like Victorian erotica. It's so precise and…" She searched her mind. "I think *delicate* is the word. Ladylike, even. Some of the erotica collections that have been published recently are good, though they tend to be too earthy for my taste. I prefer fantasy. Romance novels are wonderful. There's one historical romance writer in particular…." She wrinkled her nose, thinking hard, then smiled determinedly. "I'm sorry, her name is escaping me."

Jericho sensed that he had her backpedaling toward

the wall. A few pushes would put her up against it. "So let's get back to the actual writing—"

Madame X popped off the couch in a swirl of blue silk. "Goodness, don't y'all find this talk of mechanics dreadfully dull? The resulting book is what we should be concerned about, Jericho, darlin'. You have read *Black Velvet II*, haven't you? Why don't we talk about your favorite story?" She came around his chair, her manicured hand trailing flirtatiously across his shoulders. "Maybe there's one that suits you especially. Everyone seems to have a secret fantasy they want to discuss with Madame X."

Me and "Lacey," he immediately thought. *Naked. On a bed. That was enough.*

Aloud, he said with some discomfort, "You tell me your secrets and I'll tell you mine." It didn't feel right, having Madame X come on to him. And that was surely one for the record books.

She leaned closer. "Does your secret fantasy have anything to do with—" her golden hair swung silkily against his cheek "—my assistant, Lacey?"

He flinched. "How'd you know?"

She laughed without answering. "Shall I help you set the stage?"

Before he could answer, the assistant entered the room, unwinding a long, fringed muffler from around her neck. "It's getting really cold out there. They're talking about snow in Minnesota—" She stopped abruptly, taking in their proximity, the caftan slipping off Lacey's shoulder and the guilty look on Jericho's face. Her eyes glittered. "What's going on? No, don't tell me." Her voice was crisp and hard. "Madame X, you know you're not supposed to—"

Madame X beamed. "Good news, Lacey! Jericho has

just consented to be your escort for the formal dance we're to attend in Minneapolis tomorrow night!"

Although Jericho opened his mouth to say otherwise, when he saw the look of girlish pleasure that washed away the stiff expression on the assistant's face, he knew he couldn't disagree. And he knew that he didn't want to—no matter how disappointing her duplicity.

6

Amy Lee's arms drooped to her sides in surrender. She was weakened by lust, an astonishing, marvelous, frightening state.

The stranger's arms went around her and she sank against the broad, muscled wall of his chest with a small sound of relief. Her knees were too weak to support her weight.

Yet when he began to kiss her, she rose on tiptoes, her spirit soaring. This was all that she'd yearned for in the dark of her dreams—she would open her arms and heart and mind and step into the sensual fantasy as a full participant.

"I CAN'T BELIEVE you did that."

Lacey threw another dress from the closet onto the bed. "He likes you. You like him. You're both on the tour for the duration. Why shouldn't you have some fun together?"

"I'm not complaining, exactly." Amalie caught the next piece of clothing Lacey tossed over her shoulder. "And I'm certainly not wearing this one!"

Lacey turned to consider the garment Amalie was dangling by its shoulders. It was a form-fitting, stretch velvet cat suit, meant to be paired with a tunic or vest. "'Course not," she said, snatching it away. She folded it and dropped it into her suitcase. "This shindig is *for-*

mal.'' She flipped through the pile. "I must have something that will fit you."

Amalie checked her watch. "Twenty minutes before we have to leave for the airport. You don't have time to worry about what I'm wearing to the dance. My red dress will do, if need be."

"Lord, no. That dress is so mother-of-the-bride." Lacey sighed. "Sweetie, I swear, I'd think you had no sense of romance if I hadn't read your stories." She held up a black velvet skirt that would be six inches too long on Amalie. "Do you think we'll have time to shop in Minneapolis?"

"Have you looked at the itinerary? Minette Styles went overboard. Every minute of Madame X's time is scheduled for the next forty-eight hours."

"Let's hope there are no more Bob Slobs on the docket."

Amalie winced; she'd stood stricken outside the booth listening to the horror of that morning's radio show. "Minette admits she made a mistake there. She had no idea that Robert Pye's radio name was Bob Slob. And didn't she congratulate you on how well you handled him? She said even book-tour veterans would've been stumped."

"If only I'd been as quick with Jericho," Lacey muttered, her head in the depths of the closet. "Aha! We have a winner!" She pulled a dress out from behind their winter coats and brandished it overhead.

Amalie wasn't to be distracted by mere fashion. "What did you say about Jericho? I thought he didn't have time to ask many questions before I interrupted—and may I remind you that you should never have let him into the room in the first place?"

"It went fine, just fine." Lacey danced the dress around the room by its narrow velvet spaghetti straps, the beaded fringe at its neckline swinging to and fro. "Isn't this perfect? It's a baby-doll mini on me, but on you it'll be a classy empire-style dress down to your kneecaps."

"Much too skimpy," Amalie said, dismissing the scrap of black velvet and chiffon. "I want to know what you said to Jericho. Even a tiny slip could be important."

"You'll need a tiny slip, all right. Did you bring anything besides serviceable cotton underwear?"

"Lacey!"

Lacey sat down on the bed beside Amalie, folding her long legs beneath her, the dress in her lap. "I'll repeat every word of the interview if you promise you'll go to the dinner and dance with Jericho. No excuses."

"Fair enough." Amalie was smug, as she'd never had any intention of missing the opportunity to dance with Jericho. Lacey had underestimated Amalie's amorous inclinations.

Lacey shrugged. "Okay, I admit I had a teensy problem when Jericho started pushing me about how Madame X writes, who were her influences and all that. I recovered fast, though."

Amalie gnawed her lip worriedly. "We've gone over every possible question and answer. Victorian erotica—"

"Yep. Precise, delicate, ladylike. I fit it all in. Really, it's not a problem. Jericho probably didn't even notice that I hesitated."

"I don't know. He seems very perceptive, even though he doesn't let on how much he knows."

"Nonsense. You're being a worrywart. But…" Lacey made a please-don't-scold-me wince. "Who was that romance writer I was supposed to cite?"

"Susan Johnson."

"That's it. And such a simple name, too. I don't know how I forgot it." Ignoring Amalie's look of dread, Lacey folded the dress over her arm. "Now tell me, what do you think about this frock for the dance? It *is* a bit skimpy, so you should wear that marvelous black velvet cape against the cold."

"Absolutely not, Lacey. We specifically chose the cape for Madame X's appearances in the Midwest. You might not get the chance to use it once we travel to warmer climates."

"But I want you to wear it."

"It doesn't matter what *I* wear. You're Madame X. You're the one people will be looking at."

Lacey winked. "Jericho will be looking at you."

The thought was enough to make Amalie weaken. She did harbor a sneaking, covetous hunger to wear the hooded, floor-length, black velvet cloak—it was so elegant and theatrical. "I'm not the type," she insisted.

"You're the real Madame X, even if we're the only two who know it. I'd say that qualifies you for cape-hood at least once. I'm getting a whole closetful of new clothes out of this trip, so I won't take no for an answer."

Amalie chuckled. "We're fighting over who should be more glamorous."

Lacey stood and dropped the dress into Amalie's lap. "Let me tell you, sweetie, I'm glam enough without the cape. I'm going to be dressed in skintight, stretch black velvet with a neckline down to here." She sliced the flat of her hand down her torso and wiggled her hips. "Your only problem will be keeping Jericho's attention!"

"Oh yeah?"

Lacey tossed her hair. "Yeah!" She shoveled the remainder of her wardrobe into the suitcase in haphazard fashion. Amalie, predictably, was already packed and organized and ticking off the minutes. Lacey paused and considered her friend more seriously. "Am, I do worry about how you're dealing with the reality of me getting all this attention in your place while you get pushed aside. It must be tough when you know it's rightfully yours."

Frowning, Amalie slid her feet into a pair of flatheeled boots. Although Chicago was cold, there was no snow on the ground. Minneapolis might have both; she was going to be prepared. "It was a little strange at first," she finally said with a small sigh. "But I'm getting used to it. I always did think of 'Madame X' as a separate person from me, anyhow, you know? She's so witty and sophisticated and dramatic. And sexy—she might have actually done some of the things she's written about."

"She?"

Amalie's smile was wan. "Seeing you play Madame X has made her even more of a separate entity. She may soon take on a life of her own—I just hope I can keep her from getting into too much mischief."

"Do you ever think..." Lacey was still studying Amalie thoughtfully. "Maybe we shouldn't go through with this tour if that's going to be the result. I was hoping you'd make Madame X more a part of yourself, not less. For instance, when was the last time you had a date?"

"I date," Amalie said. *Twice a year.* "There aren't that many eligible men on Belle Isle."

"Well, thank heaven Madame X swept you out of such a state of deprivation and into a world of glamour and excitement."

Amalie grinned at that. "The old girl's a regular hurricane."

"So why don't you let her take over, just a little, during our big evening out? Jericho would appreciate it, I'm sure."

"Oh, *Jericho*," Amalie scoffed, as if he was more of a trial than a thrill.

"Tell me there's no chemistry."

Amalie hesitated. Whenever Jericho was near she felt his presence with a dizzying weakness that hit her at the back of her knees. And with a tingle that prickled across her skin like a continuous electric shock. And with a slow, sinking heat that slid from her pink cheeks all the way down between her legs so she was perpetually damp with arousal. When he wasn't around she was in nearly as poor shape—something in her was constantly seeking him, leaving her distracted and out of sorts with everyone else. She could put that down to the ordeal of concealing her secret for only so long.

Amalie pressed her fingertips to her temples. "I can't," she admitted to Lacey, as though either of them was in doubt.

"Then act on it!" Lacey slammed shut her suitcase for emphasis.

I will, Amalie vowed to herself. *I will.*

She stroked the black velvet bodice of Madame X's dress. Not someday soon, either, she decided.

Now.

SNOW SWIRLED over the distant Minneapolis skyline like confetti in a snow globe. Amalie shivered as she looked out the window of the airplane. She was a slight, thin-skinned, warm-weather creature, a product of southern seas and hot sand. She was not built for winter.

"Feeling the cold already?" Jericho asked as he slid into Lacey's abandoned seat. The handsome copilot had come back to invite her up to the cockpit ten minutes ago.

"Brrr." Amalie hugged herself, pretending the goose bumps that had popped up on her arms were from a chill and not her customary response to Jericho's vital presence. "Now I know why the *Black Velvet* book sales spiked in Minneapolis," she said, covertly studying his profile as he looked past her to the winter wonderland view out the window. His was not strictly a classic bone structure, and his expression was often too unyielding, but he was handsome nonetheless.

She couldn't quite put her finger on why. Oh, any woman would be attracted to the raw physical beauty of his toned body. And a positive feminine response to his casually confident masculinity was automatic. It was his face—his eyes in particular—that drew Amalie. She sensed there was an explosive, dynamic, hungry soul behind that cool facade and the eyes that were so remote they seemed haunted. In purely female, curious and nurturing ways, she wanted to be the one to release him from his bonds. How to do that was another matter. Not in bed, surely. Despite the unpredictability of his kisses up to now, she suspected that Jericho had already demonstrated to a long line of eager lovers just how skilled and precise and entirely in control he was in bed.

His brown lashes dipped when he looked sideways at her. "How's that?"

For a startling moment she thought he'd read her mind. Shaken, she remembered her comment about book sales and blurted out her vaguely embarrassing assumption. "Because they need something spicy to warm them up at night."

Jericho smiled. "Isn't that what the Beach Boys claimed Northern girls do for their boyfriends?" He settled back in Lacey's seat, humming under his breath. "Now, what was it they had to say about Southern girls…?"

"There should be a song rating the dubious qualities of men. Men with a reporter's credentials. Men…" She eyed his worn leather jacket. "Men in cowhide. Men who—who…" *Kiss and run,* she wanted to say, but that wasn't accurate. *Men who kiss and coolly stroll away when you're hot and bothered and screaming inside for more, more, more!*

"Careful, honey, you're running off at the mouth again."

Amalie tried to control her even more wayward thoughts. "You can call me Lacey."

"I don't know about that. Every time I do, you wince—"

"I don't wince!"

"Infinitesimally. I don't think Lacey is your real name, but I can't figure out why you'd need a fake one. Unless you're not Madame X's assistant at all."

"Not that again," Amalie croaked, seizing up inside. *He couldn't know,* she told herself. *He doesn't know, so just keep your head about you.* She looked out the window. "I'm tired of this game, Jericho."

He made a gravelly sound in his throat. "You think I like it?"

"It's what you do, isn't it? Pick and probe and pry into a person's private life until they don't have one left?"

"You signed up for this book tour of your own free will, as far as I know."

"That was my mistake," she said. "I'll probably regret it until the day I die."

Jericho could not leave that one alone. "Strongly put,

for an assistant on the periphery," he commented, sounding rightfully suspicious.

Amalie closed her eyes. "Please leave me alone."

There was such a long silence she might have thought he'd gone if she couldn't still sense him beside her, stolid yet enticingly male, warm but so cool, charming and aggravating and sexy all at once. Despite the circumstances, his presence called to her. She yearned to feel his arms wrapped protectively around her, to be able to confide in him the truth about her fears and insecurities and know that he loved her, all of her. Which was ridiculous. Long ago, when she'd been taken from Belle Isle and enrolled in a new, frighteningly proper school, she'd learned the safety of keeping to herself. One or two misadventures had been enough to teach her to keep unruly tendencies inside, even when she was itching to escape the smothering propriety of her quiet surface.

I never realized, she thought in surprise. That must be why she'd begun keeping a diary all those years ago—it was the only place she could release her pent-up feelings. And it stood to reason that as she matured and her sexual drive developed, some of the writings had become an outlet for her erotic fantasies as well.

What would happen to the uncontroversial, self-contained, subdued Amalie Dove—the only Amalie she and her small community recognized—if she was revealed as Madame X? Would she die of embarrassment, as she'd imagined, or would she be released into a wider, richer, more satisfying world?

Jericho's low voice broke through her thoughts. "I promised to be your escort for the awards dinner. And the dance afterward."

Amalie looked at him with new eyes. "Yes, you

did." *And I promised to turn my fantasies into reality—if only for one night.*

"So...?"

She cracked a smile, forgetting that she'd just told him to leave her alone. "So I hope you have something to wear besides jeans and a brown leather jacket."

MADAME X HAD BEEN INVITED to participate in a regional writers' conference, book fair and awards ceremony. Via Minette Styles, she'd accepted with pleasure, and politely insisted on extra tickets for her assistant and their escorts. Lars Torberg was filming a movie in Canada and had called when they were still in Chicago, meaning to spend his free weekend with the celebrity author who'd stolen his heart. Thus a well-dressed quartet—Lacey, Lars, Amalie and Jericho—had been ferried in a limo provided by Lars to the evening event at a conference hotel on the city outskirts.

As one of the season's hottest sellers, Madame X was given an unexpected award from a chain of Midwestern bookstores. Then she was presented a certificate of appreciation from the writers' group for her participation. And finally she was announced as the winner of the readers' choice Favorite Author trophy. By the third award, Amalie, seated at a table distant from the celebrities' dais, had learned not to flinch—even infinitesimally. She ate a spoonful of strawberry mousse and smiled at Jericho, genuinely happy that Lacey, as Madame X, was collecting such flattering accolades.

The pleasure of being with Jericho—who was wearing a tux!—may have had something to do with her equanimity.

He watched Lacey mince from the podium in her tight, mermaid-style dress, blowing kisses with theatrical joie de vivre. "The *Black Velvet* books are a phenomenon," he said flatly. "I don't quite get it."

Amalie wasn't surprised. "You're a man."

He arched his brows in an unspoken question.

"Everyone knows men prefer visual stimulation, while women like..." Although she'd started off with a pat, lecturing tone, the way that Jericho was appreciating her visuals—displayed more than she liked in Lacey's still-too-loose empire bodice, even though they'd taken a few stitches in the side seams—made Amalie's throat clutch and her words run dry. He knew how he was affecting her, too. The sweep of his lashes and slight twitch of his lips told her that he had no problem with taking it further.

Physical awareness sizzled between them like an electromagnetic field. Carefully Amalie set aside her spoon as the awards ceremony concluded and the attendees began to move to the ballroom.

"You were saying?"

She swallowed. "Women prefer to employ all their senses. They like to set the stage, take their time, draw out the romance, savor every aspect of the—the...experience. No wham, bam, thank-you-ma'ams will do."

"I can't argue that men are animals—"

Sleek, strong, beautiful, untamed male animals, Amalie thought. *And thank heaven for that.*

"—But some of us do appreciate the art of seduction."

She was too self-conscious to look him in the eye even though she was burning up inside.

"I do, for one," he said softly.

She looked. She looked so fast the faceted jet teardrops at her earlobes swung back and forth like miniature pendulums. She looked and she liked what she saw.

Jericho was a playboy bachelor and a traveling man; she knew that. And he wasn't a giver, emotionally, but then neither was she until she felt truly comfortable with a person. Perhaps his intentions were not honorable, and perhaps her heart was too involved and she would be hurt.

At the moment, she didn't care. She wanted him.

She wanted him in the back of a cab and she wanted him in the middle of a Mardi Gras masquerade ball. She wanted him on the carpet before a fireplace and she wanted him naked on a beach. She wanted him any way at all.

If she dared.

"We're supposed to move on to the dance now," Jericho said, unmoving though he remained. Hotel employees had begun to clear the tables.

Amalie plucked her small black velvet evening bag from beside her plate. Its beaded design matched the jet-bead fringe at her low neckline, the fringe that swung over her small breasts each time she moved, tantalizing them into diamond-hard peaks. She knew she should've worn a bra, but Lacey had pointed out that all the ones Amalie had packed would show beneath the narrow velvet straps and equally skimpy bodice. They certainly couldn't have that, could they?

Reluctantly Jericho stood and held out her chair. She pressed her palm between her breasts as she rose, holding the bodice in place so it wouldn't gape and treat him to a truly explicit visual.

"I expect you're not the type of man who likes to dance," she said as they stepped into the ballroom beneath an arch of silver and blue balloons. Long skeins of sheer, midnight blue organza twined with strings of blue pinpoint lights festooned the high ceiling. On the dance floor, Lacey and Lars stood out as if they'd been spotlit, their celebrated golden presence drawing every eye. Amalie was content as she was.

"It's not dancing I dislike—it's the dance itself," Jericho said, his gaze also on Lacey and Lars. "Too much glossy surface on display."

Amalie decided she was extremely content. Although the waltz music moved infectiously through her limbs, its draw could not rival her strong attraction to Jericho. The drape of his soft wool trousers and the cut of his jacket with its black velvet lapels made for a very glossy surface, and underneath was the confounding, disturbing, magnetic man who'd turned her life topsy-turvy before he'd written a word.

"We could duck out," she ventured to say.

He accepted the suggestion gratefully. "Are you sure you wouldn't mind?"

She shook her head. "How often does one have a limo at one's disposal? We can always send it back later for Lacey and Lars."

He put his hand on her arm and led her back out to the carpeted lobby, where the music and noise from the party made only a pleasant background atmosphere. "Not many women are willing to give up on a dance so easily, especially once they've dressed for the occasion." Again his gaze slipped over the brevity of her top and the shape of her legs in silky black hose and spike-heeled red sandals—impractical for the snow, but they were the only evening shoes she'd brought because they matched the red dress Lacey wouldn't let her wear.

"I'm quite the gal," Amalie joked. Her heart was in her mouth.

"You are that," he agreed, taking her hand. "Let's go

roust out the chauffeur and drive around the city and—"

"Drink champagne and look at the lights and—and…" She faltered; all she could think of was what had happened in her story "Limousine Lover," and she lacked the long, black velvet evening gloves to bring that about.

"And…" Jericho's pale eyes were heated with desire. "Make out like crazy fool kids," he said.

Amalie had no voice to answer, but her yes came through loud and clear nonetheless.

"This is just like 'Limousine Lover,'" Jericho whispered teasingly into her ear after he'd directed the driver to take the scenic route and had activated the partition that ensured their total privacy.

Ticklish, Amalie hunched her shoulders and giggled shyly. The heat hadn't kicked in yet and she was shivering beneath the velvet cloak, ready for hot chocolate rather than the glass of champagne Jericho handed her. Lars had ordered the limo stocked to meet their every decadent wish, Madame X being the type of woman who inspired such extravagance.

"So you *have* read the books," Amalie said. "Not just the good parts?"

Jericho put the bottle back in its built-in ice bucket without pouring himself a glass. "Well, yes, I read them. But I *lingered* over the good parts."

"You lingered."

His hand slid slowly over her thigh. "Despite your assumptions, some men do know how to linger."

"The best men," she whispered, setting aside her glass after one sip. She put her hand on his shoulder and shivered; the cold, fresh air still clung to his tuxedo. "You should have worn a jacket."

He caressed her bare arm, then entwined their fingers and lifted her hand to his mouth. His lips were warm and pliable. "I only brought the one and you said not to wear it."

"Why do you wear the same clothes all the time?" she asked, her eyes glazing over with the drugging wonder of the pleasure seeping through her. The car's engine hummed distantly as it sped toward the city. She felt warm now, inestimably warm.

"I hate shopping."

She wriggled closer against him, her leg curling over his thigh. "No one hates shopping that much."

"I don't like to waste time on clothes." The way he parted her velvet cloak made it seem as though he was unwrapping a precious gift. "They're unimportant. Distracting," he added with a small moan. He passed his hands over her filmy, tulip-edged chiffon overskirt and brief bodice as if to prove their insignificance. "I try not to judge people by appearances."

The beaded fringe over Amalie's breasts shivered when she did. She was on tenterhooks again, holding her breath, awaiting the touch of Jericho's lips on hers, anticipating the texture and scent and strength of his hard, bare chest beneath the glamour of his rented tuxedo. Black velvet was all well and good—and quite sensual in its place—but sometimes a man and woman had to get down to essentials.

Dazedly she said, "Wearing this dress made me feel like a whole other person."

He hesitated with his hands hovering an inch above her breasts. "But is that good? Or bad?"

"Good, because that's why I dared—oh!" Suddenly the tires screeched; the back end of the limo lurched beneath them. Amalie was thrown into Jericho almost as she'd intended, her breasts pushed hard against his palms.

The limousine slid sideways across the road with a sickening lack of control and slammed into something large and soft with a muffled *whump.* Jericho's arms went tight around her as they tumbled across the tilted leather seat, bumping chins and foreheads and knees, then came to rest in a tangled knot against the door.

A thick shower of powdery snow had blanked out the windows, leaving them stranded in a silent, chilly, padded cocoon that felt uncomfortably like a coffin.

7

Her mouth was hot and sweet. Their kisses were consuming.

She was trembling. Through his palms he felt the vibration of her body, tuned to an exquisitely expectant pitch. She steadied herself, fingertips pressed to his slick chest with the scorching sting of firebrands. Who was she? How had she so easily burned her mark as deep as his heart?

Deliberately he stepped back, his gaze raking her. With a sudden, efficient violence, he tore her sheer gown open from the neckline to the hem, leaving it in tatters that fluttered against her bare limbs. She gasped, wobbled, then again steadied herself, her eyes grown wide and alarmed. Still she did not speak.

Her body was entirely exposed. It was soft, plush, roundly feminine, her skin pearly pink in the moonlight.

His for the taking.

"ARE YOU OKAY?" Jericho asked Amalie, shifting his weight off her. Glass crunched underfoot.

"I'm fine, I think." Carefully she untangled herself and slid farther up the angled seat. She'd bumped her head, there was a nasty run in one stocking and the cape was twisted around her waist. Otherwise she was in good shape. "What happened?"

Jericho looked out his window at a bank of white nothingness. It was like being buried in an avalanche. He reached across Amalie to the button that operated the other, now higher, window. Clods of snow fell inside as it opened to a burst of cold night air.

"We must've hit a patch of ice and slid into a snowbank." He opened the partition between them and the chauffeur. "You okay up there?"

The driver unsnapped his seat belt. "Yep, I'm okay. Just couldn't do a thing when we skidded on that damn ice."

Amalie was sliding back down the seat toward Jericho. She braced her foot against the built-in bar to hold herself in place. "Where are we?"

"Less than a half mile outside the city," said the driver. "It's snowing bad."

"Do you have a car phone?" Jericho asked.

The driver was already fiddling with it. "It's dead. I'll have to walk for help. There's not going to be much traffic in this weather, I betcha."

Amalie became aware that downy flakes of snow were wafting through the open window. Several landed on her velvet cape and she examined them, deciding that they were pretty in their intricate patterns and really rather fragile—they disappeared instantly under her fingertip. Then she pulled herself up and looked outside. Wind gusted the heavy snowfall into stinging swaths and rapidly accumulating drifts that obscured the road beyond ten or fifteen yards. "This is a blizzard," she said in awe. "You can't go out in this."

The driver was a robust Northerner. "I've seen worse. Came up kinda quick, that's all. If I'da had my four-wheel drive, you'd be in Minneapolis by now." He reached for a goose-down jacket stowed on the passenger seat.

"Maybe we can dig out." Jericho pushed past Amalie and opened the door. "Let's have a look."

Snow and cold air swirled through the limo's interior as he climbed out. Amalie was no hardy soldier, but she wrapped herself up in the velvet cape, smiled bravely when Jericho poked his head back inside, and offered to take the wheel to drive them out while the men pushed. He told her to wait until they'd assessed the situation.

She pulled on the tasseled hood of the cape and sat quite still in the growing cold, listening to their muffled voices and enduring occasional thumps that rocked the limo. To occupy herself, she began picking ice cubes off the floor and dropping them back in the bucket. Fingers numb from the ice and spilled champagne, she gathered the shards of the shattered flute in a linen napkin. Disasters like this never killed the moment for the *Black Velvet* heroines, but then hadn't she known she wouldn't live up to the part?

Jericho came back. "No good," the driver said from behind him, shaking snow off his thick purple-and-gold Vikings jacket. "She's stuck something fierce."

Jericho shuddered under a light mantle of snow. Snowflakes spangled his lashes, then melted when he blinked. "We're going to walk. It's not far—"

"You're not walking wearing only a tuxedo." Amalie was aghast. "Look at you—you're already freezing!"

"She's right," the driver said, getting behind the wheel to restart the car. "Just keep the heater going and the tailpipe free of snow. I'll be back with a tow truck before you finish your champagne." He slammed the door and trudged up to the road. Within seconds, he'd disappeared into the spring snowstorm.

Amalie took Jericho's hands in her own. "Don't even

think about going after him," she warned, dipping her head to puff warm air on his fingers. "Besides, I don't want to be left alone."

"All right," he said equably, even though there were lights and signs of life close by. "I guess this isn't so bad, having a bewitching little pixie breathe on my hands while I look down her top."

Amalie gasped and dropped his hands to press her own to the front of her dress. "Your mind should be on more serious concerns," she accused, tugging at the cape until it was double wrapped across her chest. "We could suffocate, or starve, or perish from hypothermia—"

"Little danger of that. As long as we have gas, we have heat." He checked the console drawers and refrigerated compartments for provisions. "We also have a selection of capers, caviar, crackers, cheese, toast points, smoked salmon and deviled eggs." He took out a jar of nuts and offered it to Amalie. "Care for a pistachio? There's also candied almonds."

She laughed shakily. "I suppose there are worse ways to be stranded." Settling back, she nibbled a pistachio and tried not to worry. Soon her brow furrowed at the thrum of the engine. "Jericho? Are we breathing fumes from the exhaust?"

"Don't worry, we shoveled out the tailpipe." He stood and snaked his shoulders past the divider, stretching to open one of the front windows a crack. "Just in case."

"We won't be hit by another car?"

"We're in the ditch, honey, well off the road. Our only danger is being buried by a snowplow." He sat down close beside her and took her into his arms. "Just kidding, I think."

She drew back, clucking like a mother hen. "You should take off that jacket. It's wet from the snow."

"Will you keep me warm?" he asked, peeling it from his shoulders, then unknotting his tie and slipping off his cuff links for good measure.

"We can share my cape." She opened it wide and twined her arms around his neck.

"This isn't working," Jericho said a moment later. Because of the tilt of the car, they'd gradually slid down to the low end. The armrest was digging into his hip. "Let's try stretching out on the seat, with our feet against the door."

Once they were comfortably arranged under the velvet cape, Amalie snuggled cozily side-to-front against the length of Jericho and smiled. While perhaps it was simply the strangeness of being teamed against the cold in an emergency situation, she felt rather comfortable and safe with him now—though admittedly still fizzling with arousal.

"Bet you never thought the evening would end up with us horizontal quite like *this*," she said.

"This isn't horizontal—it's diagonal." His arms went around her waist to pull her even closer. "I did have an inclination to wind up draped in black velvet, though."

She muffled her laugh against his pleated shirtfront. "I hope Lacey—" *Isn't worried*, she was going to say before she stopped herself.

Jericho tilted his head back to see into her face. "What?"

Amalie's brain spun. "I...hope...lacy, uh, underwear—" her cheeks flamed, but she was desperate "—and a flimsy dress will keep me warm enough," she finished weakly.

He rubbed the see-through chiffon and whispery

black taffeta of her layered skirt between his fingers. "Lacy underwear, huh?" He put his mouth near her ear. "Not velvet?"

She couldn't believe she'd said that, and she couldn't believe he expected her to prolong the subject by admitting that black lace had been all she could find on such short notice. "We might as well use this time to get to know each other," she said with false cheer, as if a woman other than she was pressed against his body talking about her undies. "Why don't you tell me about that book you wrote? I know its title can't truly be *A Hundred and One Sneaky Reporter Tricks.*"

He hesitated, his thumb rubbing idly against her hipbone. "It was a political exposé. Do you remember the so-called Gardengate scandal a few years back?"

"Yes, of course." Gardengate had involved a tangle of greedy land developers on the verge of bankruptcy, amoral politicians, an Aussie mogul named Nigel Garden and a call girl hired by lobbyists to seduce them all. Forests had been sacrificed for the resulting reams of verbiage and investigation. "If you've been doing a Woodward and Bernstein thing," Amalie said doubtfully, "wouldn't you consider the Madame X profile a little lightweight?"

"It's an assignment. I need the money."

"Oh." She'd been brought up not to discuss personal, potentially touchy, subjects. Then again, that pertained to across-the-dinner-table conversation, not diagonal-in-the-back-seat-of-a-limousine talk. The warmth between their bodies was building and she was dying to squirm with it—which didn't seem any wiser than lapsing into an intimate conversation. Instead she said, still overbrightly, "Really, Jericho, I just realized I don't know the first thing about you. For instance, where do you live when you're not traveling for a story?"

"There's a one-bedroom apartment in New York that I visit a few times a month, but I'm planning to—" He broke off with an exasperated sigh. "Do we have to talk about this?" Beneath the cloak, Amalie felt his index finger follow the run in her stocking all the way up under the tuliped hem of her dress. She squirmed. His chest vibrated with a sexy, insinuating chuckle. "I can think of better things to do—like investigate this lacy underwear of yours."

"Just because we've been put in a compromising position..." Amalie stopped herself. Exactly why was she protesting? Hadn't she decided that she *wanted* to be compromised?

When Jericho's eyes shone they were the exact color of a sunrise screened by the pine marshes of Belle Isle. "Yes?" he prompted, almost gloating.

"I guess we do have to keep ourselves...warm," she said, measuring her words, conveniently ignoring the fact that the heater seemed to be pouring out plenty of warmth. Her blood was stirring deliciously.

"I knew you'd see it my way," he murmured, and his lips came down on hers with swift, skilled assurance.

His kisses were wonderfully thorough—all-consuming, even. Certainly her hesitation was obliterated. She shuddered and squirmed as his tongue traced the line of her throat. He murmured a compliment and kissed the tops of her breasts inside the loose, fringed neckline.

Instantly Amalie was awash with the most compelling of needs, swimming with molten desire. Unfamiliar waters—she clung to what she knew. "I'm the president of the United States," she said when Jericho momentarily lifted his mouth. "I am—*oh*." She gasped with pleasure. He'd squeezed one of her breasts lustfully, using his thumb to rub the luxurious black velvet across its acutely sensitive peak.

"You're the—" A lock of tawny hair slipped across his face when he cocked his head quizzically. His expression cleared. "Oh, right, you're the president."

"And you're a secret-service agent."

Again his hand closed over her breast. She felt as though a bolt of lightning had slashed through her—even her soles tingled. "Sworn to protect and defend and adore your delectable body under any circumstance," he said, getting into the game.

Her teeth chattered. "Ex-exactly."

"We're in the back of a limo traveling to a stodgy black-tie dinner at the French embassy when you suddenly ask if I'd like to see your underwear." Jericho swept the cape away and lifted Amalie's dress. His eyes widened, then narrowed with fevered intent. Her thighs quivered as cool air spilled across them. "I'm shocked to realize that Madame President is wearing a skimpy garter belt and the tiniest black lace panties I've ever seen." His voice was hoarse. "Even though I find you incredibly sexy, I can't allow myself to touch you. It would be improper to do so without your permission."

Amalie no longer wished to contain her imprudent inclinations. "Touch me, Jericho," she urged. "Touch me all over."

His hand went directly to the triangle of black lace, directly inside it to the dark, silken hair, and cupped her intimately, firmly, but that was all. She moaned softly and thrust herself against him, the heat and congestion of her immediate desire pooling there beneath his palm until all her years of erotic fantasy and stifled yearning were brought into sharp focus, centered on the touch of his hand between her thighs.

She clawed at his shoulders, straining upward in the raging need to be…*taken.* Taken with desire, taken far away, taken to an unknown paradise. When she looked into his smoldering eyes, any remaining vestiges of her inhibitions were burned away as she shamelessly begged for completion. *"Please."*

His hard, handsome face, held so near hers that she could not look away, did not change expression even as two of his agile fingers slipped inside her dewy warmth to find the tiny, sensitive, hidden pearl. His touch was delicate, and so piercingly exquisite her body jerked as she cried out involuntarily, her eyes still locked with his. "Easy," he murmured soothingly, while his fingertip made small, circling strokes that instructed the opposite. She writhed in his arms.

Her thighs had parted wantonly. Knees raised, she dug the spike heels of her sandals into the padded car seat and thrust up with her hips, instinctively wanting more even though she knew she couldn't possibly stand it. Surely she would die from such pleasure.…

Jericho's eyes blazed. His fingers seared her tender flesh. She remained unblinking as the first convulsive waves of her climax approached too rapidly for doubt or question. The ecstasy of it broke full force inside her and she had no choice but to succumb, her entire body quaking cataclysmically under Jericho's hand as she stared into his unwavering, sea green eyes. She was just sentient enough to reason that while female intuition told her his composure was not dispassion, he *was* a scoundrel for making her do this alone—more or less.

Finally the tremors subsided and she was able to look away, moving her cheek sensuously against the smooth leather seat as soft whimpers sounded in her throat. Though her strength was sapped, her mind was sharpening—she recognized at once that she'd moved beyond modesty, beyond playful eroticism. Even beyond intimacy.

What she felt was too strong to be anything less than love.

Anxiously she looked back at Jericho, needing something from him now, some acknowledgment, even if it was only physical.

His gaze was elsewhere. "Let's get rid of these," he said, moving his hand from the offending panties to the straps of the first garter Amalie had ever worn. No doubt he was more experienced than she at undoing them, but as renewed desire surged through her she found that her impatience to have him inside her wouldn't let her wait.

"Rip them," she urged most recklessly, not surprised to hear that her voice sounded quite different. Everything about her had changed in the past few minutes.

"Yes," Jericho said quickly, the insistent throbbing of his rock-hard erection reason enough to agree. The task was not as easy as he'd supposed. He had to balance himself above her in the confining space and yank so hard her slim hips lifted off the seat. At last the panties ripped and he tugged them from beneath the straps of the matching garter. He dropped the scraps of black lace on the car floor.

Snowflakes drifted out of the blue-black night beyond the car window. Lacey-who-was-not-Lacey's eyes had closed indolently, her dark lashes like feather-fine strokes of an ink pen against the rosy blush of her cheeks. He was startled by his tender regard for her, and without analyzing his motives he moved quickly to disrupt the quiet intimacy, unzipping his pants and spreading her legs with an impatient motion before she could speak.

Her eyelids flew up. Her luscious mouth gaped. "Oh!" she said with not-disapproving surprise, though he didn't let her get another word out. He reached down with his hand to open her wider and with a smooth, practiced lunge buried himself hilt deep inside her moist, clinging flesh.

He hesitated then, panting raggedly, his hair hanging in disarray.

She took a deep breath and put her hands on his chest, then lifted her legs, her tight inner muscles flexing provocatively. "*Jericho*," she breathed, marveling. "It's all right. It's wonderful...."

A loud groan burst from his throat; he was no longer in control. There was something uncommonly disturbing about making love with this woman, yet she was so soft and silky and lithe beneath him, and warm and wet around him, that he couldn't hold back long enough to decide what exactly was wrong. He couldn't hold back any more than he'd managed to staunch his growing ardor.

With gentle hands she drew him down to her. "Touch me." She kissed him, her lips sweet, her tongue bold. "Touch me deep inside."

He braced one foot against the door and dug the other knee into the seat and used all the power of his thickly muscled thighs to thrust hard up into her. She caught her breath, her lashes fluttering. The flat of one of her hands skimmed down his back to the hollow of his buttock; his skin burned under her touch. "Yes, like that," she whispered, reaching up to curl her fingers around the door handle.

Jericho felt desperate, frenzied. With his hands behind her knees to lever them higher so he could go as deep as possible, he drove hungrily into her again and again. He was rapacious, using his physicality to blur the curious yearnings of his heart. Yet when he heard the tremulous cries of her climax and answered them with his own explosive release, it was with so strong a sense of affection that all his denials were belied.

He sank beside her, spent but not satisfied, still stubbornly refusing what was obvious even though his hands were loving as they drew the black velvet cloak around her petite body. Confronted as he was by a maelstrom of emotion that refused to be tamped back down, the best he could do was to concentrate on keeping her warm. So he closed his eyes and hugged her tight and tried to stop himself from feeling anything that was not strictly physical.

8

The wave broke over the beach with a soft *whoosh*, reaching as far as Amy Lee's hips. The contrast between the cool surf, the wet sand and her hot flesh was shockingly erotic. Her hips rocked from side to side; her belly squirmed deeper into the slick satin sand.

Even though she couldn't see the stranger's face, her body reacted automatically to the heat of his gaze and the wordless pressure of his hand on her stomach. Her pelvis tilted up again as the surf receded, and she was acutely aware of how she must look on her belly before him with her round bottom bare and upthrust, stark white in the moonlight.

When she heard the sound of his zipper, she cradled her head in her arms. The sand was gritty on her lips and cheek. At least she didn't have to watch her own mindless, irrevocable surrender to decadence....

JERICHO'S HOTEL ROOM was ordinary.

And it was the most beautiful thing Amalie had ever seen.

"I thought I'd never be warm again," she said from her nest of blankets on the double bed, and shivered at the remembered cold. "I despise snow."

"You're a spoiled baby." Jericho put their empty

hot-chocolate mugs on the room-service tray and got back into bed, obviously eager to warm her up again. She had no objections.

He snaked his arms under her swaddled layers. "We had heat till the tow truck arrived. Your only exposure to the snow was the ten seconds it took me to walk from the limo to the truck and the five feet of frozen sidewalk between the curb and the hotel."

"I was wearing *sandals*," she said, appalled, though her spine tingled with the memory of Jericho sweeping her up into his arms the instant she'd poked her foot out the door, struggling manfully out of the ditch through shin-high snow and depositing her in the cab of the tow truck. It had been such an heroic act, she almost hadn't minded that her torn panties had dropped out of his pocket in the process and lain against the snow in crumpled black-lace testimony to his *other* act of heroism.

They'd transferred back into the limo after it had been pulled from the ditch unharmed, and had eventually reached the hotel in one piece, though Amalie had sworn she couldn't feel her feet so she couldn't be quite sure. She'd taken a hot shower, counted her toes, wrapped herself in the hotel's complimentary white terry robe and buried herself under a mound of blankets, complaining noisily all the while.

"You need taking care of," said Jericho. She was rosily nude beneath the robe, not cold at all.

Amalie, known for being responsible and self-sufficient at home on Belle Isle, smiled to herself. She could get used to being pampered now and then. "You take very good care of me," she purred, amazed at how easily lover's play came to her in so short a time. It wasn't experience; her few relationships had not been memorable in that aspect—or any other. Perhaps it was simply because being with Jericho felt so right. "I could easily grow accustomed to it."

He did not answer at once, and she knew she'd gone a little too far. "So could I," he said at last, though the admission seemed grudging to Amalie's ear.

She chose to concentrate on solid ground. Or solid chest. Unfortunately, because of all the blankets, she couldn't get a good look at his and had to content herself with seeing by touch, sliding her palms along the sleek, curved contours of muscle and bone until she found the furry patch at its center, tracing her nails across his washboard abs, discovering the hypersensitivity of his pebbled nipples when she nipped at them.

A desire to speak of love was growing inside her. *Too much,* she reminded herself, and closed her eyes to conjure up a scene. "It's the time of the midnight sun," she said huskily, her heart not really involved.

Jericho hesitated, perhaps because he discerned her underlying tone. He gave no other notice if he had. "Northern Alaska," he countered, parting her robe, his knuckles brushing against the sides of her breasts. "An igloo."

"The ice walls are luminous. They glow with a pale, eerie light." She rolled onto her back. "The air is close with the scent of wood smoke."

He moved over her, his weight propped on his elbows. "When I arrived by dogsled, the man of the family offered me the use of his wife, as is the custom, but my preference is for his eldest daughter. Even though she stays in the background, quiet and obedient, there is mischief in her eyes."

Amalie began to sink into the blissful aura of seduction. Perhaps it was enough. Jericho's face was all confident masculinity above hers, his stomach flat and hard against her belly, the velvety head of his penis probing her damp cleft with frisson-inducing prowess.

"They finally sleep, and I come to you, naked under the furs," she whispered. "I know you're waiting for me."

His palms curved appreciatively around her breasts. "I couldn't sleep. Your exotic ways have enchanted me." He took one of her nipples into his mouth and suckled it until she felt the delicious ache as deep as her womb.

Amalie's mind whirled. Suddenly she was adrift, not certain if she was speaking of fantasy or reality. "I've been waiting for you all my life."

"You're so willing, so satiny warm," he said. The muscles in his shoulders rippled under her hands as he shifted to rest his forearms on either side of her. "I find it so easy to slide up inside you."

The slow, cleaving glide of his rigid shaft was an excruciating lesson in delayed gratification. She was as open as a full-blown hothouse rose, and still he made her wait for it, inch by tantalizing inch. She hugged him tighter, burying her face against his chest as he described every sensation, every action—hot, erotic, sexy words that made her tremble with frustrated passion.

"I've waited for you," she panted. Her eyes were wild. "I've dreamed of this for too long."

"I'm here." He slid the last exquisite half inch inside her, their bodies slippery in the heat they'd generated under the thick mantle of blankets. "I'm here at last."

She tightened around him, her fingernails raking his shoulders. He filled her snugly, yet still there was inside her a gnawing need for more. "You won't stay," she said, straining to hold back the extent of her desire.

"I can't." His hands covered her breasts as he surged between her widespread thighs.

"I know." One anguished cry tore free from her throat before she managed to turn her head and bite down on the pillow instead as bittersweet rapture engulfed her. The liquid fire of orgasm flooded her loins; his, hers, theirs—no difference, no separation.

When it was over, she took Jericho's face between her palms and made a soft promise. "You'll go away soon, I know. But until you do, I'm yours." She was careful not to use his name. He wouldn't know for certain that she was speaking not of their fantasy but of the truth.

JERICHO WAS SHAKEN.

Once she had finally drifted into sleep, he left their bed to move restlessly about the room. He should never have listened to Harry, should never have taken this job. Obviously, he should never, never have made love to Lacey or Emily or whatever her damn name was!

He looked at the small hump she made under the blankets. The ruffled layers of her short dark hair were all that showed. She wasn't like any of the other women he'd shared beds with so casually. Mistress of erotica or not, she was too innocent and trusting to have learned that sex could exist strictly for enjoyment—it didn't have to mean so much.

It didn't have to mean anything at all.

He thought specifically of Delia Banks for the first time in years. She had taught him that lesson when he was sixteen and too stupid to know that Miss Cordelia Banks of the East Hampton Bankses was only interested in one thing from a nobody with little to recommend him except a naive teenage admiration and a body that had matured too soon into a state of untutored sex appeal. She'd led him on, she'd used him, and when the heat got too high, she'd dropped him without compunction.

Suddenly Jericho remembered the look on his step-father's face when the president of the country club informed him of what Jericho had been caught doing with Delia Banks in the smoking room. It should have become a laughable mishap after all these years.

It hadn't. Dispassionately Jericho looked at himself in the shadowed mirror over the bureau. He moved closer, noticing two months too late that his hair was getting long—he would get it cut before he appeared in East Hampton or risk his parents' disdain. They'd already made it clear on their infrequent meetings that they felt he'd turned into a no-account vagabond.

The thought of returning disturbed Jericho; he looked for a distraction. He touched the keys of his laptop computer where it rested on the bureau. Madame X. He was close to solving her mystery.

Again his gaze returned to the bed, to the woman whose name was still undetermined. She sighed sweetly in her sleep, a vulnerable sound that stirred his emotions.

He wasn't supposed to have emotions, especially as far as an assignment was concerned.

Madame X was his assignment. The assistant was—

What if the "assistant" *was* Madame X? What then?

He swore softly, his glance falling on her evening clothes scattered across the rug. Knowing what his intentions were even as he casually picked up the dress and the black velvet cape, he paused to hold them to his nose and inhale the intoxicating, elusive fragrance of a desirable woman. He thought of how she'd looked wearing them—like a naughty, bewitching pixie-sorceress. When he tossed the garments over the back of a chair, the jet-bead fringe clicked softly, as it had each time she'd moved and the neckline gaped and he'd caught another enticing glimpse of her perfect ivory breasts with their tiny, perky nipples.

The hell with it, he thought abruptly, stamping out another rush of affection by taking heedless action. He picked up her small purse—the snap had already popped open though that didn't negate his culpability—and reached inside. Mascara, lipstick, folding money, her driver's license. Her driver's license.

Jericho examined it in the dim light from the window. Not Emily, he realized at once. *Amalie, Amalie Dove.*

Beaufort Drive.

Belle Isle, South Carolina.

MORNING CAME as it always did, albeit a morning unlike any Amalie had known. It was a cold, clear, blue morning outside their hotel window. Crystalline flecks in the long white drifts of undisturbed snow glittered in the sunshine. Inside, it was a warm, cozy morning with a man, a handsome man she knew intimately yet scarcely at all, a man who was, shockingly, her lover.

Not that he was acting like one. Since she'd wakened, he'd been on the phone, ordering breakfast, making business calls. She took a shower—wishing Jericho was with her—and slipped into the white terry robe, crumpled black velvet not being appropriate even on a morning like no other.

A huge breakfast arrived on a castered, room-service table, and Jericho, still on the phone, motioned for Amalie to eat while it was hot. She sat reluctantly, wishing he was with her. It sounded as though he was talking to a real estate agent, and she was just comfortable enough with her new role to think that the purchase of even coveted beachfront acreage could wait.

Jericho hadn't kissed her good morning, she realized poutingly.

Maybe it wasn't a good morning after all.

What had been a vast appetite was shrinking, but she heaped her plate with a wedge of cantaloupe, half an omelette, three strips of bacon and a minitower of silver dollar pancakes. Her eyes flashed at Jericho—who was this Debbie person and why did he sound so friendly toward her?—and then she attacked her breakfast.

Other than chemistry, you have no reason to love him, she scolded herself. Pretty spectacular chemistry, yes, but everyone knew how quickly that burned out. Most likely she was mistaking lust for love—having a limited experience with either.

Why, then, did her heart ache when she glimpsed the hurt behind his haunted eyes and withdrawn expressions? Why did the thought of being with him fill her with not only desire but also sweet, gooey affection and the need to prolong the attachment indefinitely? Why did she want him out of bed as much as in?

She knew almost nothing about him. And he wasn't offering to illuminate her. Even during their night together, when the openness inherent in sex had been known to breach many an emotional wall, Jericho had revealed little of himself.

Except in the touch of his hand and the taste of his kiss, she thought, melting at the memory. Surely a man who made love so exquisitely was not entirely uninvolved?

She crunched a strip of bacon, glumly admitting that she just didn't know how these things worked. Was there a protocol for new lovers?

At last Jericho joined her, his apology perfunctory. "Sorry."

She hacked at the melon. "You're in the market for

beachfront property?'' she asked idly, keeping all her eagerness inside as she thought of the long, warm, private beaches of Belle Isle. She must keep a clear head. Just because their bodies had merged did not mean their lives were going to.

Just because she'd fallen in love with him did not mean he'd fallen in love with her.

"I'm leaving today to close the deal."

Amalie almost choked. "You're *leaving*—"

"This afternoon, I hope. If I can get a flight."

"Oh." She bit her lip. "Well...I guess that means you're finished with Madame X."

Calmly he cut into the omelette. "Not quite."

Although Amalie held her shoulders stiffly, her hand shook as she clutched the lapels of her robe. "May I ask what that means?"

Jericho stared. "It means I'm not finished with you."

She blanched. "M-me?"

"Amalie Dove," he said, his voice soft but lethal.

She closed her eyes in silent prayer as her small, ordered, self-contained world crashed spectacularly around her.

9

The night air was ripe with the scent of desire. As the ocean lapped at their intertwined legs, the hot, biting kisses of Amy Lee's fantasy man traveled up the twisting length of her spine. He nipped at her shoulder, her neck, his hands reaching around to fill themselves with the opulence of her swaying breasts. Amy Lee's head drooped as the last bit of strength drained out of her braced arms.

He kept one brown hand clamped over her breast and twisted the other through her hair, exerting an easy pressure with both until she was all the way up on her knees, her arched back thrusting her derriere against the distended, pulsing flesh of his erection. She begged softly for the consummation it promised.

THIS IS THE END, Amalie thought in despair. It was useless to evade. Even if Jericho didn't yet know every detail of the scheme, he could easily find out now that he had her name.

Words came with a struggle. "You...know. How did you—"

"I'll be honest," he said. "I looked at your driver's license."

Her heart turned to stone. "Was that why you seduced me?" she rasped. "To gain access?" She went on recklessly. "Pity I wasn't also identified as Madame X to save you the trouble of further investigation. I suppose next you'll be after Lacey." Her hand flew to cover her indiscriminate mouth, but it was too late. Much too late.

"Don't worry," Jericho said. "I already know the blonde's name is Lacey Longwood."

The blank calm of his stare across the table was more disturbing to her than anger. Such a bloodless confrontation was light years away from... She glanced at the bed. What *had* happened between them last night? Had they made love or had they simply played out a nasty little game of masquerades?

"What all do you know?" she asked.

"You tell me."

She stood and paced across the room, biting her lip, glancing at him warily. "I'll make you a deal," she finally offered, having decided that at the very least she could gain a little knowledge of her own out of this debacle. "I'll answer questions if you'll answer them, too."

Uncertainty flitted over Jericho's features. "What do you mean?"

"It's little enough to ask. I'll give you your damn Madame X profile if you'll satisfy my curiosity." She stopped pacing and looked him in the eye, long practice in containing herself coming in handy. She couldn't let him see how deep her feelings went. "I do like to know the basic facts about the men I sleep with."

"Fine." He flipped his hand as if her request was of no consequence. "First, tell me about the name, or names, if you prefer. Let's get all your identities straight."

Amalie wanted to sit, but she wasn't going to be fro-

zen in place across the table from his icy countenance
and she certainly wasn't going to plunk herself on the
rumpled bed. She pulled out a spare wooden desk
chair. "As you already discovered with one of your
sneaky reporter tricks, my name is Amalie Dove. My
friend is Lacey Longwood."

"And which of you is Madame X?"

Her eyes narrowed. "You don't know?"

"I have a pretty good idea. I had someone look up
the incorporation papers for Black Velvet, Inc., the
copyright holder listed in your books. That was one of
the calls I placed this morning. My researcher told me
that Amalie Dove is the president of the corporation—
surprise, surprise."

"Yes," Amalie whispered.

Jericho's eyebrows arched.

"Yes," she said, louder and a bit angrily. "I am Madame X." Her hands clenched. There, she'd said it, and
it had been even worse than she'd imagined. No surge
of newfound freedom or flood of relief arrived to wash
her clean of the guilt and evasiveness of the past
weeks.

"So now it's your turn," she charged, hiding her
misery well. "Tell me about *your* name, Mr. Thomas
Janes Jericho. Now that we've made lo—well, uh, do I
now get to call you Thomas? Tom? Maybe Tommy?"

While his shrug was nonchalant, she sensed tension.
"My name's no big deal. I use Janes professionally in
honor of my maternal grandparents, who were always
there for me. Jericho was my father's surname, but I
didn't know him. He was a working-class man who
died when I was a baby."

"Mmm." Amalie pressed her lips together, trying to
figure out what he was withholding. "Does anyone call
you Tom?"

He remained unmoved. "My mother calls me Thomas. My stepfather doesn't call me anything except 'your son.'"

"Your son? That doesn't make sense."

Jericho looked away. "He says it to my mother. As in 'Your son always was a good-for-nothing.'" When Amalie murmured consolingly, he shook his head, dismissing the subject. "Forget it. Let's talk about your books."

Back to her, unfortunately. She frowned. "What do you want to know?"

"Why did you write them? Why did you publish them?"

She squirmed on the hard chair. "Why not?"

"'Tryst,'" Jericho announced, suddenly remembering. "I suspected that story in particular was significant, and now that I know your name I see why. Amalie Dove. *Amy Lee Starling.* Beaufort Drive, Belle Isle. *Bellefort Island.*" He cocked his head. "Any other similarities?"

And here she'd thought she'd been so clever. "Sure," she snapped. "I'm always running down to the beach to meet anonymous lovers." She jumped up and started pacing again. "Don't you get it, Jericho? It's all fantasy, including Madame X. The name of the real author isn't important. Having Lacey make appearances in my place was a lark, not a mean-spirited fraud."

"Norris Yount and Rosie Bass agree?"

Amalie groaned. He would ask that.

"They don't know, do they?"

"I...didn't tell them." Maybe she could still make Jericho understand. He might even agree not to reveal her identity if she told him everything—Senator Dove included. Then again, it was possible she'd only be digging herself deeper. "There could be ramifications that go beyond me," she explained, then spun quickly and sank onto the bed. "You have to understand that this wasn't a well thought out plan. For reasons of my own, I used a pseudonym, with intentions of keeping my private life separate from the professional. But then when the second book was to be published, Pebble-pond wanted to use my photo on the jacket. I couldn't give them my own, so I sent them one of Lacey instead. With her permission, of course. She thought it was a—a caper."

Amalie looked up, smiling wanly; Jericho didn't respond. "All the rest—" her arms waved "—the interviews, the book tour…well, they just sort of happened."

"Uh-huh. That's what they all say."

Amalie snorted. "I haven't committed any crimes on the scale of Gardengate!"

"It's something of a swindle nonetheless."

He was a stickler, she saw. He wasn't going to let her get away with a thing. "Equal time," she said stubbornly. "Your turn to answer the same questions. Why do you write what you do?"

"Because I think frauds and cheats should be exposed. Because the face many people show to the world is not the truth." He shrugged. "Because books, even frivolous books of erotica, shouldn't be judged strictly by their covers."

Amalie's eyes darkened. If that was how he felt, he must find her despicable now that she'd admitted lying to him all along—and for such a "frivolous" cause. There seemed little hope of salvaging their relationship. If one could call it that. How quickly they'd gone from hot sex to cold comfort. She blinked and sniffed and asked, "But *why* do you feel that way?"

Jericho waited too long to give his simple answer;

Amalie's curiosity ripened even through her despair. "I happened to see a lot of two-faced posturing when I was growing up. I didn't like it."

"So you went to journalism school and became a plainspoken crusader for the common man?"

He laughed harshly. "Not right off. I bummed around for a while before I finally decided to do something constructive with my life." His eyes flickered. "And I'm not immune to indulging in the trappings of success."

"Like beachfront property on Long Island?"

"That's right." Suddenly he stood, clanged various covers back over the plates and dishes of their half-eaten breakfast and shoved the table toward the door with excessive force.

Amalie was silent for a long while, contemplating her situation. She could say little, do nothing, and still be exposed on the cover of *NewsProfile*. Or she could spill all her secrets and trust that Jericho would treat her fairly—maybe even more than fairly if he had any feelings for her whatsoever. And he must, she decided, thinking of how he'd kissed her, how he'd touched her. Surely he must.

She sat up straighter and tightened the belt of her robe. "Thomas Janes Jericho," she said, using the full name because she didn't quite dare to call him anything less. "I'm going to trust you."

He frowned and raked his hands through his tawny hair, standing barefoot before her in the usual white cotton shirt and jeans. Her pronouncement seemed to make him uncomfortable.

She took the plunge anyway. "Maybe you've heard of Senator Barbara Dove of South Carolina."

"Of course." He smacked his hand against his thigh;

obviously he figured he should have deduced a possible connection himself. "Any relation?"

"She's my mother." *He would have found out anyway*, Amalie told herself, hoping against hope that there was a trace of compassion inside Jericho. And that he was worthy of the gamble.

"I see. And you think acknowledging your authorship of the *Black Velvet* books will harm Senator Dove's reputation?"

"In some voters' eyes, yes, it certainly will. I'd hoped to spare my mother the hassle. And myself the notoriety." Amalie winced, imagining the worst. "Senator Dove's constituency is basically conservative. I suspect they won't take kindly to my news. And the occupants of Belle Isle are rather stodgy—they resist change. They won't welcome an invasion of mainlanders from the media."

"You're in a bind, then," Jericho said quietly, and sat beside her.

Amalie fingered her lapels, acutely conscious that she was nude beneath the one thin layer of terry cloth. "Especially as I'm a little on the stodgy side myself." She exhaled, her stomach already so aflutter with agitated butterflies she didn't dare gauge Jericho's reaction to her confession.

He leaned his elbows on his knees. "Let me guess." He nodded to himself, looking down at his clasped hands. "You're asking me not to print the truth about Madame X."

Impulsively Amalie grabbed his arm. "I know I shouldn't, but you must realize what will happen. The publicity would be devastating. My life would never be the same." She hesitated, wondering why that no longer seemed like the worst result, then realized it was because she'd already been altered beyond repair.

"If there were other reporters who were suspicious, or if I thought I *had* perpetuated a swindle, I wouldn't ask you to kill the story, Jericho. As things stand, though, I just don't see how ruining my life, and maybe wrecking my mother's career in the process, will prove anything. No one but you cares that Lacey isn't the real Madame X!"

He turned his face toward hers. "Not even you, Amalie?"

She froze. "Of course I care."

"You know what I mean." He put his hands on her shoulders; her spirits lifted, blindly optimistic. "Remember, I have firsthand knowledge of how your fantasy life works, honey. I know how deeply you feel. If you're not entirely a shrinking violet—and you're not—then there must be some part of you that would like to take hold of Madame X and run wild with her." He paused, waiting for her to meet his eyes. "Amalie, you *are* Madame X."

"Not the one Norris Yount hoped for." She licked her lips. "Not the one the public expects."

"So what?"

"So…I don't know. I really don't know what to do next, Jericho. I wish there were directions I could follow."

"Well, number one, you can call me Tom, if you'd like."

She laughed nervously, her eyes glistening with tears. "Uh, hey, Tom?"

"Yup?"

"I think I prefer Jericho. At least until your walls come tumbling down."

"What's that supposed to mean?" he asked, but she could see that he knew. Still, she wasn't going to push it. There was the sheen of emotion in his eyes for the first time that morning—soft, natural, caring emotion—and she didn't think that he even knew it.

She found the courage to brush her cheek against his hand. "It means that number two is a kiss, because I want to know that you forgive me for lying to you."

"I forgive you." He hesitated. "But don't ask me to make any promises about—"

She hushed him with a finger to his lips. "Let's just leave that for now."

He inhaled deeply, his eyes closed, his Adam's apple working up and down in his throat. "I don't know if I can."

Exactly what Amalie had been afraid of. Her fledgling sense of daring deflated.

Number three, she thought, drawing away from him. *I still love you.*

"GOR-JUSS, BABY, absolutely gorgeous. Do it to me, yeah, like that, ooh, I want it, babycakes, you gorgeous thing, you."

Thank heaven that's not me—yet, Amalie told herself, trying to block out the photographer's nauseating patter while she watched Lacey preen and pose under the hot lights. Amalie would feel like a bug squirming under a magnifying glass if she was put in the same position, but Lacey had taken to the photography session like a seasoned pro. In fact, she'd handled every aspect of the Madame X role with aplomb.

And she did look gorgeous, moving like a panther in the same gown she'd worn to the awards banquet, the sheen of its stretch black velvet shifting under the lights as her sleek, curvaceous body flowed from position to position. She stretched out across a white silk, gilt-legged chaise, arching her back off the cushions, breasts rounding in the slash neckline, throat extending as she let her head fall back, lustrous hair spilling like a golden waterfall as she smiled upside down at the camera.

The epitome of a mistress of erotica.

And still a lie. Amalie grimaced, picturing herself on the cover of *NewsProfile,* sitting stiffly on the edge of the same lounge chair, wearing one of her pretty, ladylike outfits, her hands folded in her lap, a deer-in-the-headlights look in her eye. The word *Fraud* would be stamped across her face in big red letters. And written across the bottom of the page: "By Thomas Janes Jericho."

"Fantastic, Madame X." The photographer snatched a fresh camera out of the hands of one of his assistants. "Now let's get down on all fours—ooh, yeah, you're an animal! Gimme some attitude, gorgeous."

Amalie turned and headed for the coffee urn set up on a table at the back of the studio. She took a cupful, trying to convince herself that since today's session hadn't been cancelled by *NewsProfile* it meant Jericho wasn't going through with the story. He hadn't given her a clue about his intentions before catching an afternoon flight back to New York, so Amalie was carrying on as if nothing had happened. She could hardly call a halt in the middle of the book tour on the mere possibility of exposure.

"Hot stuff, huh?"

Amalie looked up. Lil Wingo, Jericho's photographer friend, was hovering near the remains of the lunch buffet. She picked a slice of cucumber out of a leftover sandwich and popped it into her mouth. "Turbo's a big toad in a little pond. Still, he knows how to light cleavage."

Amalie smiled tentatively. "Forgive me for sounding naive, but I thought you were going to be handling the cover shoot instead of this Turbo guy. Aren't you *NewsProfile*'s photographer?"

"I don't do much studio work." Lil's face was narrow and sharp, her expression discerning but friendly. She was too scruffy in her baggy chinos and ragged, crew neck sweater to be intimidating. "I'm really just a jumped-up paparazzo, but Jericho and I work well together."

"You work together often?"

Lil plucked a slice of shaved ham from a different sandwich, shook it, tilted her head back and dropped it in her open mouth. "Maybe six, eight times a year," she said, chewing.

To be companionable, Amalie chose a cherry tomato pierced by a toothpick. "So you know him well."

"No one knows Jericho well."

The warm tomato slid off the toothpick and into a tub of half-eaten chicken salad. "I kind of got that feeling," Amalie murmured.

"Yeah, and he *likes* you."

Her head snapped up. "How can you tell?"

"C'mon," Lil scoffed, and her expression said that she knew exactly what had happened between Jericho and Amalie the previous night.

"Beyond that." Amalie's cheeks were hot, but she had to know.

Lil squinted thoughtfully. "Dunno if there is a 'beyond that' with Jericho."

Amalie's shoulders slumped; she abandoned the squishy tomato where it lay and walked toward the corner of the room through the shadows cast by the studio props, her head down. She tried to appear deep in thought, should anyone be looking. In reality she just didn't want them to see her crumpled face.

After a few minutes, Lil wandered by. "A word to

the wise, little sis. Don't be looking for more with Jericho. He's a nice guy, for sure, but every time you think you're getting somewhere with him, he closes up tighter than a clam."

"That's no way to live," Amalie said thickly. Not for herself, either, she realized.

"I'm a rolling stone, myself." Lil shrugged. "So's Jericho, but I'm not convinced he really wants to be."

Amalie found a tissue in her purse and blew her nose into it. That was better; she edged out from behind a roll of backdrop paper and looked Lil in the eye. "He's gone to buy some property in the Hamptons, you know. That sounds pretty stable to me."

For once, Lil was taken aback. "Is that so? The Hamptons, you say?" She plunged her hands into her loose pockets. "I'll be damned."

"He didn't tell you about it?"

"Sort of. A couple years back we were on some island or other covering a CIA-sponsored uprising and he got drunk enough on Tiki Hurricanes to let a few things slip."

"Such as?" Amalie held her breath.

"He grew up mainly in East Hampton. You ever been there? Wall-to-wall richniks, not my kind of place."

"Or Jericho's," said Amalie, more confused than ever.

"You got that right." Lil crunched a potato chip she'd found clinging to the sleeve of her sweater. "I guess Jericho's stepfather was your typical monster-slash-mogul and his mother had turned herself into a WASPier-than-WASP ice princess to please the sugar daddy who'd snatched her out of the pink-collar ghetto. Jericho was a rebel—he didn't fit their self-important image."

"Oh, gosh." Amalie remembered everything he'd said about two-faced people, about truth and deception and justice.

"So I'm kinda surprised about him going back there."

"Maybe he has a good reason." Amalie sighed deeply. *And maybe he has plenty of reason to want to publicize the plain truth about Madame X, too.* She was beginning to understand that it was all of a piece.

"Hey, looks like Turbo's wrapping up." Lil unwound the strap of her camera from around her neck. "I'm going to shoot a few frames of the group for posterity—you want to get in the picture?"

"No," Amalie said, much too emphatically. She covered up with a smile. "No, thank you, Lil. I'm one of those people who hates to have her photo taken."

"No problem." Lil swung around, figuring she'd find some other way to sneak a few shots of Madame X's assistant, as Jericho had requested in a private consultation earlier that day. Though she'd teased him a little about wanting photos of his latest paramour, the hard cut of his jaw and the coolness of his eyes had made it clear that his intentions were other than romantic.

Lil glanced back at the girl who was in love with him. Poor kid.

IT WAS ANOTHER WEEK before Amalie made it home to Belle Isle. As the ferry chugged into the small harbor, she felt both relieved and apprehensive—grateful to be back, yes, but more than a little worried that soon her home would never be the same. And the blame rightfully lay at her door.

The island encompassed only three square miles in its entirety, and it was less than one mile to the Dove family home on the eastern shore. Amalie left her luggage at the harbor manager's shack near the pier and walked, waving greetings to those she recognized, which was everyone but several out-of-season tourists, but being careful not to slow down to chat. She wasn't ready to answer questions about her "vacation."

By the time she reached Southsea Road, where the houses were set back from the road and spaced farther apart, the sun had properly soaked its warmth into her bones. She slowed, slipping easily into the languid rhythm of island life. The air was soft and sweet with spring, the road beneath her feet pungent with warm tar. Yellow jessamine grew in thickets; cordgrass rustled in the breeze. Already the lavender wisteria growing on the low stone walls that bordered the road was beginning to bloom.

By all rights, Amalie should have been at peace—and she wasn't. Not at all.

Perhaps what she needed was the sight of home. She quickened her step in anticipation, yet even as she turned onto the oyster-shell surface of Beaufort Drive and passed through the shadows of the huge live oaks that lined the road, all she heard was Jericho's accusatory voice saying, "Beaufort Drive, Belle Isle. Bellefort Island." *Amalie Dove, Amy Lee Starling.*

She shook her head in a futile effort to dislodge his presence. There'd been no word from him; Lil, too, had moved on after the cover shoot. The rest of the book tour had proceeded without major incident—by then, minor disturbances like reporters angling for juicy details and mash notes from male readers didn't faze either Lacey or Amalie. The people at Pebblepond Press were delighted with the favorable publicity and soaring sales the Madame X campaign had engendered.

Only Amalie suffered under the knowledge that the whole house of cards could collapse at any moment.

She knew she should inform Norris and Rosie. And prepare her parents, giving her mother's staff time to work out a plan for damage control. There was no way to shield Belle Isle from what could come, but surely Lacey deserved advance warning. She was likely to be ridiculed for her part in the charade.

If Jericho went through with it. Amalie was delaying all action in the hope that he might not publish the story.

Bells rang in the near distance and her spirits leaped. She was home, no longer the girl she'd been, it was true, but she was home!

Though one could see the Atlantic from the rise of Beaufort Drive, Amalie's gaze was on the large, sun-bleached green, Gothic Revival house that had always been her home. Ancient wisteria vines clogged the long porch roof, and above their dense green-and-purple mass several steep-pitched, weatherbeaten gables peaked sharply against the deepening sky. The dinner gong sounded once more, propelling Amalie up the steps and through the tall, triangular-topped front doors.

"Marydoe," she called. Her voice echoed through the cool, shadowy foyer. "I'm home!"

The housekeeper came down the back hallway, drying her hands on her apron. "Amalie Jane—I declare! Why didn't you call ahead to let me know?"

"You rang the dinner gong and I smell sweet potato pie—you must've known I was coming, anyway." Amalie hugged Marydoe warmly.

The housekeeper's smooth brown face creased in a smile. "You know I always ring the bells, even when it's just me and John at home. That's the way your granddaddy wanted it and that's the way it's done." She patted the cocoa-colored puff of her bun, proud as always that she hadn't been caught slacking off.

Amalie had relished the sound of the bells. She'd grown up at their direction, compliantly following the dictates of the morning bells, breakfast bells, naptime bells, dinner bells, sunset bells and evening bells. Sometimes even rowdy-kids-dangling-on-the-rope bells.

She hugged Marydoe again. "It's really good to be home. I suppose my parents are in Washington?"

Marydoe nodded. "They left me in charge."

As if there'd been any doubt, Amalie thought fondly. Mary Dorothy Davis was of Gullah descent. Her ancestors had been born on Belle Isle and never budged an inch; she still spoke the Gullah dialect on occasion. She was fifty-three, and had always been too tart and disciplined to be the kind of motherly house-keeper who'd coo over the oftentimes lonely daughter of the house and bring her cookies and milk in bed. Marydoe wasn't a tireless, selfless saint with a soft lap and an unbending ear, yet for all of that she had be-come Amalie's very good friend over the years. Partly because she could be relied on to give a kindly swat when it was called for and a straight answer when it was needed.

"Look at you, young'un. You're thin as a rail. Didn't you find any Yankee food to your liking while you were traipsing around the country with Lacey Eliza-beth?"

Amalie followed Marydoe along the passageway to the kitchen. She'd told her family that she was accom-panying Lacey on a book tour, concocting the story that her college friend-turned-actress had been hired by the publishers to portray Madame X in order to explain the upcoming publicity.

"I ate cheese steaks in Philadelphia, stuffed pizza in Chicago and something startlingly fishy in Seattle," Amalie said, "but none of it tasted as good as home cooking."

"Set yourself down, Amalie Jane. I'll see to it your stomach is filled." Marydoe went to the stove and stirred the she-crab soup the way she had for as long as Amalie could remember. The wooden spoon and her place on the pine floor had both been worn satin smooth over the years.

John, the caretaker and groundskeeper, came in the back door. "Miss Amalie, how do?" he said, beaming. He slid a tweed cap off his bald, freckled head and nodded at Marydoe. "Evenin', Miss Marydoe."

"Evenin', John. Don't you track mud on my floor."

"Now, how could I do that when I ain't been near the mud?"

Amalie sat at the wooden kitchen table, watching happily as Marydoe fussed at John and he tolerated it with a winsome smile. Amalie, Ruby and Charlie used to embarrass Moses to death speculating on the relationship between his mother, the widowed Marydoe, and bachelor John, but if there'd ever been a romance they gave no sign of it save talking back and forth like an old married couple.

"How's Moses doing?" Amalie asked, once the food was on the table.

The housekeeper jumped up, remembering the pickled okra. "He's doing well, far as *I* know—and that's not very far. Says he's coming home for a visit in a few days and I've got a bad feeling. Think he's planning to tell me he's divorcing that woman of his."

Amalie and John exchanged a grin. Marydoe had

been predicting a divorce ever since Moses married in his second year of law school—already five years ago. *Same as ever,* Amalie thought, and, somewhat comforted that her upcoming scandal wouldn't change Belle Isle as easily as that, she settled down to dinner.

Later, after Amalie had eaten two pieces of sweet potato pie, loaded the dishwasher, taken delivery of her luggage from Chick Garrity and changed into jeans and an old sweatshirt, she walked out to the beach. She was out of sorts again, and the feeling refused to go away.

She plunked herself down in the sand and stared at the dusky ocean, doing her best to concentrate on the cool breeze carrying the sour undertone of the salt marsh, or the brown pelican diving for mullet, or the never-ending constancy of the waves sweeping the gray sand. She refused to think of Jericho. She wouldn't worry over the blank look on his face when he'd said goodbye, remember how he'd driven her crazy with his touch, or ask herself why this one man had been the fulfillment of all her fantasies.

She wouldn't think of Jericho and touch her lips as he had done; she wouldn't rub her palm over her aching nipples; she would not imagine him emerging from the sea wearing nothing but a pair of clinging cutoffs and taking her right here in the sand with her eyes wide open and her body shuddering and her heart full of love....

Amalie made a sound of frustration and fell back flat on the beach, digging her fingers into the sand. Overhead the first tiny diamond stars of the evening pinpricked the darkened sky. Where was Jericho? she wondered. Was he thinking of her?

"ONE LAST LOOK," he said, "before I sign the papers."

Debbie Howell shrugged and parked the car; she

was used to going along with whatever crazy notion her clients came up with, even checking out a property in the dark.

"This isn't a case of buyer's remorse?" she asked lightly as they climbed out of her shiny new BMW sedan. She patted the hood fondly, then rubbed the spot with her sleeve just in case she'd left a smear.

Jericho didn't bother answering her question or going inside the house. Instead, he circled the property with long, agitated strides, more interested in the view next door than in what was soon to be his own inground swimming pool, flagstone terrace and straggly, haphazardly winterized garden. The Vanderveer cousins had taken the deck chairs—indeed, they'd stripped the house of everything that was movable.

"Yoo-hoo!" Debbie called from somewhere behind him. "Jericho-o-o?"

He sat in the cold sand on the beach. "Give me a minute, won't you, Deb?"

"All righty," she said, her voice floating down to him, "take your time. If you have any questions, I'll be back at the car."

Jericho glanced over his shoulder as she tottered on her high heels around the corner of the house. Debbie had gained a few pounds since high school, and learned how to dress. While she was very career-gal-about-town now, she'd let him know that she still liked hoodlums, even reformed ones. In turn, Jericho had let her know that he wasn't interested, perhaps more bluntly than he should have, because he wasn't feeling exactly social these days.

Poor Debbie thought he was having second thoughts about the transaction, but it wasn't the Vanderveer house or its vast mortgage that was eating at him. He stared at DeWitt and Betsy's place through the growing gloom. It wasn't even living next door to his parents and anticipating their reaction to the news with a churning in his gut.

No, it was Amalie Dove who lay heavy on his conscience.

Yesterday he'd turned the first draft of the Madame X article in to Harry Bass, who'd been gleeful with anticipation at *NewsProfile*'s potential coup. Lil had culled a few photos of Amalie out of the immense collection taken of Lacey, including a moody portrait she'd sneaked at the photo studio when Amalie was unaware that the camera lens had been pointed at her.

Sneaked. Not a good word for him to use when he could still hear Amalie's broachful *"A Hundred and One Sneaky Reporter Tricks"* echoing in his brain.

He was dreading phoning her to inform her of the article's impending publication and to ask for her reaction. Yet he had to give her a chance to defend herself for the record, even though she'd already illuminated her reasons for the charade back in that Minneapolis hotel room. The ethical implications of the situation were a bit tricky. Was a confession given by a woman in a bathrobe whom he'd just made love to admissible into public record?

It was still a dog-eat-dog world, right? he asked himself. Amalie had chosen with plenty of forethought to play the game, even if her intentions were not greedy or malicious.

Right. Jericho's gaze flitted over the Parishes' closed-up house. Although he'd spent his summers there in between increasing periods of banishment to his grandparents' inland cottage, he had no particular reaction to the sight of it. It was just a house, another overpriced, cedar-sided, six-bedroom East Hampton beach house that had been redecorated every other summer along with its inhabitants—out with the Hockney paintings, in with the Picasso prints, out with Art Deco, in with French Country, out with Lacroix, in with Donna Karan, out with Swiss almond mocha, in with espresso, out with the flashy Maserati, in with an old-money Bentley. And on and on and on.

Jericho stood and wiped his hands on the backside of his jeans. His butt was cold. His heart was colder.

He turned to study the frigid, charcoal ocean and pictured Amalie instead, running down a beach of warm silken sand and aquamarine water, her eyes lit from within, her pink lips forming that cute, pixieish, three-cornered smile of hers. The one that made him want to kiss her forever. *Not in this lifetime,* he thought, and regret lanced his gut.

Was Amalie back home on Belle Isle by now? Was she hating him for what he was about to do to her?

10

He filled her magnificently.

There'd always been this hollowness inside Amy Lee—a waiting for something to happen, a yearning for the undefined. She'd known one day she'd understand what was lacking. One day her dreams would be fulfilled.

This man, a total stranger even now, was not offering love. She recognized that. Still, there was reverence in the caress of his hands on her breasts, grace in the masterful thrust that reached so deep inside her, shameless beauty in the fusion of their naked bodies. He'd pierced her protective bubble. Somehow, strangely, he'd satisfied the empty space in her heart.

"HELLO, Dove residence."

"I'm calling for Amalie Dove."

"J-Jericho?"

"*Amalie.*"

Suddenly she couldn't find her voice.

"Are you there?" he asked.

Her hands were shaking; she had to use both to hold on to the telephone receiver. "I'm here."

"How are you?" He sounded tired.

"I'm…" She knew she should say fine. "Lonely." Several heartbeats passed and he didn't respond, so she added, "And how're you?" in a breathless voice.

"Lonely, too."

"Oh. Oh, Jericho—"

He cut in. "This is a professional call."

Her heart clenched.

"I need to know your official reaction to the article," he said. "It's going to run one week from tomorrow."

"You mean—"

"Yeah. Sorry, Amalie, but you have eight days to set your house in order."

She wanted to throw the phone across the room. "You're going to ruin my life and the lives of several innocent people and all you can say is 'Sorry, Amalie'?"

"I don't think I'm the one to blame." His voice was flat and hard now.

She gathered herself, knowing he was right even as an immense sense of disappointment that after ten days apart he'd called her only for professional reasons forced her to blame him for *something*. "You had a choice in the matter," she insisted. "Defrauding Madame X isn't of global importance, after all."

"Do you have a response?"

She seethed at his apparent objectivity. "No comment."

"So that's that."

He was about to hang up! "Jericho..." she yelped.

"Yes."

She didn't know what to say.

He cleared his throat and asked quietly, "Do you hate me, Amalie?"

She closed her eyes to the harsh sunlight streaming through the trefoil bay windows and said, "Yeah, I do." But her voice was as soft as rabbit fur.

"Are you going to Pebblepond's party at the Bookcon?"

Blood drained from Amalie's face; the National Booksellers Convention—Bookcon—was Lacey's last official commitment as Madame X. Now Amalie would have to show up beforehand and confess her lie to Norris Yount in person so Pebblepond Press could come up with a way to save face. "I expect so," she told Jericho grudgingly. "It's Madame X's last hurrah." Literally.

"I've been invited. I won't go, if you'd rather I didn't."

Even with all the problems he'd caused, her heart leaped at the thought of seeing him again. "Please," she whispered.

He swore under his breath, taking her plea the wrong way. "I have to go. I want to—"

"I need to—"

"—See you," he said.

She pressed her lips to the mouthpiece. *"Yes."*

"I AM MADAME X."

Lacey had covered her face with her hands, but over the scarlet tips of her fingernails, she was watching Amalie make the confession, as if this was a train wreck at which she couldn't resist peeking.

Norris Yount pinched the bridge of his nose and said nothing, no doubt hoping Amalie would shut up and go away.

Rosie Bass shook her head. "Come again?"

"I am Madame X."

They were standing in the elegant terrazzo foyer of the suite where Pebblepond Press's Bookcon party was about to begin. The caterer's white-jacketed employees darted back and forth beyond the arched opening to the main room, carrying trays of crystal and silver, arranging chairs, fussing with flowers.

The silver-haired publisher's nostrils flared. "That can't be."

Rosie looked from Amalie to Lacey and back again. "Somehow, I'm not as surprised as you, Norris."

"It gets worse," Amalie said miserably. "There was a reporter following us on the book tour, and, well, *NewsProfile* is about to tell the world the whole story. About me. About everything."

Rosie's eyes narrowed. "*Harry!* Why, that sonova—"

"Now is not the time to harangue your ex-husband," Yount interrupted. "We've got a serious problem on our hands."

"Harry's gonna have a serious problem when I get my hands on him," Rosie muttered. "He sicced that reporter after us on purpose."

"We must assess the situation." Yount's gaze caught on the artful construction of Lacey's strapless black velvet number. He looked at Amalie, in her lavender suit and pearls. "If you're Madame X, then who—"

"Lacey Longwood. I know we've put you in an awful situation, Norris, darlin', but Amalie and I had the best of intentions." Lacey smiled her best Marilyn, making sultry eyes at him beneath half-lowered lids; Yount was suitably mesmerized. "We're truly sorry it's turned out this way. If there's anything we can do…"

"I can take full blame, for one thing," Amalie said. "When the story gets out, I'll be sure to say that I did this on my own and that Pebblepond Press knew nothing about it."

When he transferred his attention to Amalie, Yount's brows arched haughtily. "No. We'd look like fools."

Rosie agreed. "We need to call in Minette Styles. She handled the PR for *Black Velvet II*. She might have suggestions for where we go from here."

Yount was staring at the bustle of the expensive

party preparations. "How could you do this to me at the absolute worst moment?" he demanded of Amalie.

She winced. "I did try to get an appointment earlier, but your secretary said you were too busy...."

"*Why* did you do this?" asked Rosie, with a kinder inflection.

Amalie waved her hands. "Look at me." She gestured at Lacey. "Look at her. I figured Lacey fit the Madame X mold better than I ever could."

"Nonsense," Rosie said. "There was no Madame X mold—at least not until you mailed us that glamour shot of a gorgeous blond bombshell."

Norris gazed at Lacey regretfully. "She was perfect, though, wasn't she, Rosie?"

"Nonsense," the editor said again. "Oh, I admit we got a lot of mileage out of her looks, but the book was selling phenomenally even before we sent Madame X on the road."

"We've got an entire booth at the convention devoted to Madame X," Yount interjected. "We just shipped ten thousand copies with her photo on the jacket. What are we going to do? How can we explain this—this..." Amalie shrank under his glare.

"I suggest holding off on the recriminations until you're sure they're warranted." Rosie patted his arm consolingly. "I may have an idea, but first let's get you a drink, Norris." She prodded him through the archway and down the steps into the suite, then glanced over her shoulder at Lacey and Amalie. "Follow me, girls. We'll need both of you if we're going to have a chance of cutting *NewsProfile* off at the knees."

AFTER EVERYTHING that had happened—which mainly meant Amalie—Jericho found himself right back where the masquerade had started: attending another glitzy party rife with ego and artifice. Norris Yount was nouveaux riche trying to act like old money; his wife was a former Rockette turned snob. Their functions were made up of as many celebrities and social climbers as writers and editors. A good portion of the guests read one book a year—the one that became a blockbuster movie. Cynically Jericho decided that they probably didn't finish even that one because halfway through they realized they could see the movie instead.

He grimaced and set aside the glass of chardonnay one of the waiters had thrust at him. The chance to see Amalie was the only reason he'd come. He'd put up with socialites feigning ennui as they talked loudly about wintering in Palm Beach; he'd put up with financiers wearing goatees and Rolex watches. All for the chance to look into her sexy-innocent, purple-blue eyes again.

Lacey was here, still dressed in black velvet, he noted as they waved at each other across the room. She seemed friendly enough, even though she had to know he was responsible for spoiling her Madame X gig.

Impatiently Jericho scanned the suite. The party was so large it had overflowed into several rooms. A writer desperate for a three-book contract chased his editor into the john. In his rush to get to Lacey, Lars Torberg bumped a nebbish who'd won the Booker Prize up against a fitness guru promoting her exercise book by wearing a spandex glove. They exchanged cards. The crystal chandeliers tinkled from the escalating vibrations of chatter about liposuction, Stephen King's print runs and which publisher was sleeping with which editor and which editor was sleeping with which writer.

Jericho blocked it all out as he watched Lars squeeze Lacey's black velvet curves in an enthusiastic bear hug.

Was it possible that Amalie was still keeping her identity a secret? As it stood, Harry Bass didn't know that his star reporter had given the Madame X camp advance warning to the extent that he had. If Harry showed up at the party to gloat to Rosie about his coup...well, fireworks could ensue.

"Here you are," said a light, feminine voice behind Jericho. Amalie leaned her chin on his shoulder. "Prowling the edges of the party, twitching your whiskers at the guests." She plucked at his loose sleeve. "Underdressed as usual." Rubbing the silky fabric between thumb and forefinger, she took in the French cut and band collar. "Wow. This is not your regular white shirt, it's your *dress-up* white shirt. Somebody shopped, and in Europe, I'd guess."

He was amazed that she was so relaxed. He wasn't. "A Frenchwoman gave it to me. Her name was Fabienne. She was a chanteuse, I think, but then we only met the once—in a barn."

After an instant of hot jealousy, Amalie recognized the reference to one of her *Black Velvet* stories. She punched him in the ribs. "No Madame X jokes, please. Certainly not from you."

"You seem..."

"I'm feeling no pain. I've drunk too much champagne." She giggled. "That was a rhyme, wasn't it? Well, almost."

Uh-oh, he thought.

Amalie slid her hands into the back pockets of Jericho's jeans. His muscles clenched. "Umm," she whispered in his ear. "Did I ever tell you that your thighs look magnificent in tight blue jeans?"

"Those aren't my thighs you've got a hold of, honey." He tried to walk out from beneath her provocative grip, but she followed behind him, giggling and stepping on his heels in a perversely tantalizing game of follow-the-leader.

Several of the party guests were beginning to notice, although in Jericho's estimation Amalie's antics were tame compared to the lewd goings-on that had been known to occur at these kind of parties. A woman in overdone sequins lifted her thinly drawn brows, raising his ire in equal proportions. The difference was, of course, that Amalie was a nobody, an outsider, and thus eligible for ridicule.

He reached back and handcuffed her wrists. "Let's go for a short walk, shall we?" With Amalie clinging to his side, he elbowed his way to the door and found a small anteroom off the foyer that was being used as a coat check.

Amalie sank onto a love seat heaped with furs. "I'm not drunk. But I wish I was."

"You've told Yount the truth," Jericho guessed.

She blinked and nodded. "Yep, and you don't want to know what they're gonna do about it." Patting the couch, she cooed, "So come on over here and give me a little kiss to cheer me up before the guillotine falls."

He sat. Maybe not drunk, he thought, but certainly tipsy. She was sprawling across the furs in an un-Amalielike manner, her skirt hiked up to her thighs, her ankles turned over like a little girl's. "Not drunk," she insisted at his perusal. Her lower lip trembled. "Just scared."

He leaned in to give her a tiny kiss. It wasn't tiny enough, though; the contact pierced him like a stiletto. He pulled back and tugged at his tight collar. "Lacey looks like she's handling it."

Amalie gripped the front of his shirt and pulled him closer. He had no choice but to put his arms around her. "Lacey loves this stuff, whereas *I* should've never left Belle Isle."

She smelled like wildflowers baking in the sunshine. He inhaled deeply. "Then we wouldn't have met...."

Her fingernails tickled the back of his neck. "Yes, that's compensation," she agreed.

"Not punishment?"

"Maybe that, too." Her back arched above his palm as she drew him even closer. They were inches away from a full-fledged recline. "Lovely, lovely punishment."

He shocked himself by saying, "I want to be more to you than that."

Her eyes widened. She started to speak, stopped, swallowed, then finally croaked, "Are you serious?"

"Yes, I think so." But he hadn't thought about it—not specifically. He was skilled at avoiding such introspection. All he knew was that he'd missed her like crazy and he couldn't take the chance that she'd slip out of his life again. If that was the first step to commitment—*Whoa!* said a voice inside that he ignored—then so be it.

Amalie kissed him. "You have to *know* it." She kissed him again, her lips light as pinfeathers but her mouth so warm he wanted to dive in and spend the night. "You have to mean it, Jericho. You have to believe it."

He remained silent even though his body was sending very loud, very insistent messages to his brain.

"I may have misled you," she continued. "I'm not really this woman who makes love in the back of limousines and invites men into her hotel room and—"

"Yes, you are. You're Madame X, remember?" He kissed her fiercely, before she could object, and soon their passion had risen precipitously and their kisses were coming so fast and furious neither one of them remembered where they were or what they'd been talking about.

"I am Madame X," Amalie said, panting raggedly while Jericho kissed and licked and sucked at the skin revealed by each button he undid down the front of her blouse. "I am a world-famous author and you are a reporter seducing me for nefarious purposes." She moved sinuously against him, rubbing the inside of her thigh over the seam of his jeans, feeling the heat of his skin and the firm musculature of his leg through the soft denim. He slipped his hand into her bra and she moaned, her nipple puckering as he rolled it against his palm.

"We're in your dressing room." His mouth sought her breast. "And your husband just drove up."

"He's calling for me." Her hand lowered to the thickness straining against his fly. "You'll have to sneak out the back way."

Jericho groaned. "I can't stop."

"All right, but be darn fast about it." Feverishly Amalie tugged the tails of his cream silk shirt out of his jeans. "I can hear him at the door—"

The door to the anteroom opened on cue. For an instant both Amalie and Jericho thought the man who stepped inside was part of their game. He, however, wasn't playing by their rules; his expression was truly horrified.

A blond woman came in on his heels. "Thomas!" she said, shock further tightening her already tightly face-lifted and overtanned skin. A silver fox fur slithered out of her grip.

Her husband pursed his lips in distaste and stiffly averted his face. "I can see your son hasn't changed."

Amalie knew who they were even before Jericho's

eyes turned to ice. He levered himself off her and turned to face them with his shirttail providentially hanging loose. "Hey, what do you know, just like the time with Delia Banks," he said, heavy on the sarcasm. "Whoops, I guess you caught me again."

DeWitt Parish sucked air through his nostrils. "I fail to find this amusing."

"How could you, Thomas?" wailed Betsy.

Jericho's thin-lipped grin was deadly.

Amalie buttoned her blouse, watching them from the corners of her eyes. DeWitt Parish looked nothing like his name. He was short and thick through the middle, with big yellow teeth and a full head of fussily sculpted white hair. He took his wife firmly by the elbow. "Tell your son to get a haircut. He looks like a hooligan."

Betsy nodded obediently. "You really should see to it, Thomas. It's much too long." She was five or six inches taller than her husband, so bone thin and desiccated that her six-thousand-dollar designer dress hung off her shoulders like a gunnysack.

"No time to chat?" Jericho asked as they quickly departed. Betsy managed a short wave before the door slammed shut. Jericho flinched, then stiffened. After a moment, he turned to Amalie, his face a mask. "Well, that was fun."

She wasn't happy with his behavior. "You didn't have to act like such a jerk. They had good reason to be shocked at our behavior." She pressed her palms to her cheeks. "I don't know what I was thinking."

With a careless air, he sprawled on the love seat, looped his arms around her hips and pulled her over to him. "You weren't thinking—at least not with your head." The flat of one of his hands slid upward between her thighs, the other squeezed her buttock. By the look on his face he could have been testing produce in a supermarket rather than fondling a woman.

Disliking the motives behind his advance, Amalie pushed his hand away. "Stop that." She thought he'd been remote before, but that had been puppy-dog friendly compared to this stony withdrawal. "I've never seen you quite so—so...what's wrong with you? You could at least have been minimally polite and introduced us."

"You wanted to meet the Commodity King and the Social X Ray? Trust me, Amalie, they're not worth it."

She touched his shoulder; muscles were bunched like small boulders under his skin. He gave no notice. "Look, Jericho..." She searched her mind, but there didn't seem to be any magic words that would make it all right for him. His walls were too tall for her to scale, too thick for her to break. She gave up with a sigh. "I guess I'd better go back to the party."

Much as she hated to, she left him sitting there and walked to the door. "You know, I could use your support, Jericho. My life is about to change."

Though he turned his head to look at her, his face exhibited no real feeling or even curiosity, so she stepped outside and closed the door behind her, hoping against hope that one day he'd realize that he did care. A relationship built on erotic fantasies wasn't enough, for either of them.

Take it from Madame X, she thought bleakly, entering the foyer. The party sounds assailed her at once, reminding her of the earlier apprehension that had made her drink too much champagne. In her distraught state of mind, that strategy appeared to be a good idea. After snaring a fresh glass from one of the white-jacketed waiters, she descended the terrazzo steps and lost herself in the crowd.

Not well enough. Within minutes, Lacey had spotted her. "Amalie, where've you been? Norris wants to introduce us to some of the guests."

Amalie glanced over and saw the publisher standing with the *New York Express* critic who'd been so enamored with Lacey's version of Madame X. "Not yet," she moaned, feeling like warmed-up leftovers.

Lacey clucked. "The first time is bound to be the worst." She squeezed Amalie's hand. "Who knows? You may even get to like being known as the woman behind Madame X."

Childishly Amalie dragged her feet as they made their way over to the Pebblepond Press publisher, scuffing the toes of her new high-heeled pumps on the carpet. "Rosie!" Lacey trilled, waving the editor over to join them.

Why not? Amalie asked herself, tossing back the champagne. The more the merrier. If she was going to perform, it may as well be in front of a crowd.

Still, she was far from prepared when it became clear that Norris Yount intended to veer from Rosie's original plan. He was supposed to gradually introduce Amalie into the party's collective consciousness until it seemed that Pebblepond Press had never intended to keep her a secret, that Lacey's Madame X had been only a publicity gimmick. Instead, Yount urged Lacey, Amalie and the editor up the steps so they stood framed by the tall archway of the foyer, elevated above the party guests. Lacey basked in the attention as heads turned, and even Rosie appeared to be in brisk good spirits despite the change in plans. Only Amalie cringed, wadding the hem of her suit jacket with her damp palms.

"Three lovely ladies," Norris said to the crowd at large. He made a sweeping gesture with his arm.

"What say we applaud the women behind Pebble-pond's latest bestseller, *Black Velvet II!*"

Amalie edged backward while the guests clapped politely. Maybe Yount didn't intend to single her out.

"First, we have Rosie Bass, my number one editor. You all know Rosie." Next, Norris took Lacey's hand and kissed it. "And this is Miss Lacey Longwood—or Madame X, as she's been known to the public. Hasn't she done a wonderful job of promoting the books for us? We couldn't have chosen a better actress." The guests buzzed among themselves, casting curious glances at Lacey, though mostly they seemed to smile and shrug in agreement.

"Now, this last lady is rather shy. Rosie and I had to persuade her to reveal herself tonight—at long last." Norris stepped up beside Amalie and nudged her toward the front. She could see that despite his smooth presentation he was still disgruntled with her. Covering well, he clasped her hand like a courtier and presented her to the speculating party-goers. "My dear guests, I give you Miss Amalie Dove, the genuine author of the *Black Velvet* books." Under his breath, he added, "Smile if it kills you."

Straining for a pleasant expression, Amalie stared out over the crowd. She saw raised eyebrows, couldn't-care-less blinks, one or two looks of admiration. The paparazzi aimed their cameras—Lil among them, smiling and chewing and shooting at the same time. There was the *Express* book critic, gesticulating wildly, his mouth open. Harry Bass, Jericho's editor, steaming off to one side. Lars Torberg, glacially dumbstruck. Betsy Parish, her hollow cheeks working like a bellows as she hyperventilated. And DeWitt Parish, sneering.

Amalie's eyes veered back to DeWitt. He *was* a roach, not worth the time of day.

Lacey applauded. "See, you're a hit," she said into Amalie's ear.

Futilely Amalie searched for Jericho. She was here because of him, but apparently he didn't care. Shrugging off the disappointment in favor of her long overdue acknowledgment, she took another step forward. "Hello," she said, her voice wobbly. "It's me, Amalie Dove." Was it the bubbles from the champagne or was she starting to enjoy this, if only in a desperate, clutchy, better-than-nothing way?

"I am Madame X," she announced grandly, and stepped forward into nothingness.

Jericho appeared from nowhere to save her from an ungainly tumble down the stone steps. He caught her around the waist and swung her up into his arms just as she realized she'd forgotten the short stairway. A few gasps came from the gathered guests, and catcalls. Flashbulbs popped. Several women broke into spiteful titters over such a graceless display.

Betsy Parish appeared at the front of the crowd, her scrawny neck so strained it looked like it'd been strung with piano wire. "Thomas, really!" she admonished.

"Tell your son to put her down," DeWitt chided. "Those awful books of hers—she's not our kind."

Amalie blinked, still stunned at her rapid ascent, but not displeased to have landed in such strong arms. She looked up into a pair of unrevealing, pale green eyes. "Jericho?"

He smiled tightly. "Now that you've made your entrance, Madame X, why don't we make our exit?"

He carried her out of the party to a round of growing applause.

11

He lost himself in her tight, liquid warmth.

Impaled with no other recourse—and apparently wishing none—she closed her thighs around the surging power of his lower body as her pliant tissues stretched to take his entire length. He drove deeper yet, watching with hungry eyes the helpless roll of her head and erotic swing of her moonlit breasts above an arching rib cage. Arms outstretched sacrificially, she searched for purchase, raking her fingers through the sand, leaving deep gouges. He was so ferocious in his passion that with each thrust their bodies bucked, inching inexorably up the slope of the beach; her soft backside would be as abraded as his knees.

His hands clamped her hips, holding her in place as instinct and pleasure and pain wound tighter and tighter within him. She writhed with bursting ecstacy, the sensuous curves of her belly and hips jumping under his touch.

His own release was explosive, profligate... addictive.

AS A QUICK GETAWAY out of Manhattan seemed momentarily advisable, Jericho offered to drive Amalie out to Long Island to see his new house. It being the kind of spur-of-the-moment adventure Madame X would approve of, Amalie readily agreed. She'd worry about consequences later.

On the way, he told her the story of Delia Banks and the Baystone Country Club scandal. "She was an older woman—twenty-one. I was sixteen, too dumb to know that I was being used. Or maybe I did know, I just didn't care because she was so hot. And wild. I thought I'd died and gone to heaven." His fingers tightened on the steering wheel. "Turned out it was hell."

He was actually talking about himself for once, so Amalie was leery of interrupting. "Your stepfather caught you...?" she prodded delicately.

"It was the president of the country club who walked in on us—one of those stuffy, cigar-smoking, old-money, school-tie types. Delia liked dangerous sex, so we were doing it in the club's smoking room during one of their tea dances. When Delia put on a show of crocodile tears, the prez decided to take into account her impeccable family lineage and my bad reputation and recommend that her name be kept out of the incident while I was kicked out of the club for good. Which was the last straw for DeWitt Parish— he'd worked damn hard to get into that country club and didn't want his own membership put in jeopardy."

"I imagine he wouldn't listen to your side."

Jericho shrugged. "I didn't have a side. Yes, I was naive and foolish, and maybe Delia and I should've shared equal blame. Still, I did it. I got caught. End of story."

Not quite, Amalie thought, knowing he still suffered the repercussions even though they'd been channeled into his journalistic search for truth and justice. She felt sorrow for the teenage Jericho, who'd probably ached for his stepfather's love and respect but was even now too stubborn to admit it. At the same time, inappropriately, she was taken with a fleeting fantasy: a dark, smoky room, Jericho in a leather armchair with his pants around his ankles. And herself, naked under her dress, seated atop him with her legs hanging out over the sides, her hips circling, slowly circling....

Amalie's head snapped back. She had to get control of her imagination! This Madame X stuff was becoming an obsession—unless it was Jericho who was the obsession. She glanced sideways at him, her insides running with a warmth that was hard to ignore while she searched for a less intimate topic.

"I made a fool of myself tonight," she said as the car cruised along the Montauk Highway toward the Hamptons, then surprised herself by laughing. "Terrible things always happen to me whenever I'm forced to be the center of attention. My first day in a new school, I went to the blackboard with the back of my skirt tucked in my underpants. At graduation, I was the one who knocked off my mortarboard when I flipped the tassel to the other side. Every time I give a presentation before the museum board, I'm bound to have a coughing fit or a projector failure." Suddenly giddily voluble, she snuggled under the creased cowhide of Jericho's jacket. "I should've known that my introduction as Madame X would end as badly."

"It wasn't so terrible. Kind of spectacular, in fact."

She laughed again. "The intention was to be subtle."

Jericho smiled ruefully. "Anyway, it's a good thing I got out of there before Harry caught up with me. You realize that Norris Yount's announcement nullifies *NewsProfile*'s impending scoop."

"Are you in trouble, then?"

He took her hand. "I'll survive."

They were passing a graveyard, coming to East

Hampton. Even though the first signs of impending spring had appeared, the village still looked cold and deserted—unlike Amalie's heart. At the touch of Jericho's hand, her giddiness had eased into a warm sense of well-being. "Thank you for rescuing me," she said. "Thank you for being there."

"Sure," he said shortly, and was quiet until directing the car between a pair of massive fieldstone gateposts. Unlike the rest of the shuttered, locked and practically barricaded estates, the tall, wrought-iron gates of this one stood wide open. A long pebbled driveway curved toward a large gray shingled house with white trim, a wide porch and a cupola. "This is it," Jericho said.

"It's big," Amalie blurted. "For one person, I mean."

"True." He frowned. "But they say location is everything." He motioned over the steering wheel at the modern, cedar-planked house next door, barely visible between the clipped hedges and a phalanx of manicured cedars. "There's DeWitt's homage to conspicuous consumption."

Amalie looked at him strangely, then left the car and walked around it toward the terrace, hugging herself beneath the unzipped jacket. "I don't understand you, Jericho. I really don't." She swung around when he came up behind her, his gaze lifted to the Parish chimneys. "The way you acted, I'd have thought you'd want to live as far away from your parents as possible." She narrowed her eyes, trying to see his expression in the dark. "Doesn't this strike you as the slightest bit perverse?"

"I didn't think about it that way."

She tapped her heel on the flagstones. "Maybe it's time you did."

"Hell," he said pithily, and grabbed her hand. "Let's go inside."

The house was vast and totally empty. Their footsteps echoed as he showed her through a few of the downstairs rooms, brushing off her questions about the rest of the space. "I've only been upstairs once," he finally admitted.

"Once!" Amalie exclaimed. They were in the immense living room, where a row of tall windows faced the black hole of the empty pool and the stone terrace with steps that led down to the beach. The ocean was the color of indigo ink, slashed here and there by the icy froth of whitecaps.

"Why would anyone buy a house they care so little about?" she demanded.

Jericho shrugged. "Isn't buying a house what everyone does once their career has become financially successful?"

"Most people put more thought into the purchase." She shivered in the chilly air, staring at blank walls, dusty floorboards and bare wires sticking out of the ceiling where once a chandelier must have hung. "What are you going to do with this place? It needs light and warmth and children—" She broke off as neatly as if her voice had been sliced with a machete.

"And a wife?"

Jericho's eyes glittered in the dim wash of moonlight; Amalie's skin crawled. Was his intention provocative? Malicious? Or possibly...? "I—I wouldn't presume," she stammered.

Casually he stretched his arms overhead, then lowered them to shake out the remaining stiffness. "I may be coming around to the logic of having one." He moved quickly across the room toward her and she jumped back before realizing that his destination was the fieldstone fireplace. A few charred logs had been left in the andirons.

Amalie pulled his jacket tighter around herself. "Good luck finding a woman who welcomes a logical proposal."

"You wouldn't?" He was squatting on his haunches before the fireplace, snapping kindling; he didn't look around.

She was momentarily safe in allowing her intense longing to show on her face. "I believe in love."

His silence was so deep she could hear the first faint hisses and crackles of the fire. "We need more wood," he said abruptly. "I'll check outside."

She shed his jacket as if it were alive and walked to the windows to rest her forehead against a cool pane. What if Jericho was one of those men who never shared his feelings? Who could never bring himself to speak of love even while it was present in his actions? Could she live with that?

The circle she traced on the fogged glass looked like a wedding ring. She drew another, interlocking them. So Jericho saw the *logic* in acquiring a wife. Perhaps he intended to choose one with all the forethought he'd put into acquiring this house.

He came back with a couple of logs and a blanket from the trunk of his car. Hastily she wiped the ring symbols from the glass. When she turned, the fire was crackling and Jericho was smoothing wrinkles from the blanket he'd arranged on the heart-pine floor before the hearth.

Spreading her palms before the flames, she acted as though it was the promise of toasty warmth that had drawn her over. She sat beside him on the blanket because there were no chairs. And when he lay on his side and curled his arm around her waist, why, only a woman with a spine of steel could have resisted relaxing against him.

"I must be back at Bookcon no later than tomorrow morning, to sign books at Pebblepond's booth." Amalie's voice was indolent. Not even the prospect of public humiliation could entirely disturb her growing languor. "And I'm on a flight home the day after. I have to tell my parents...." She sighed, not wanting to think about all of that.

"I'll get you to New York on time," promised Jericho. Lazily he petted the slope of her hip.

She turned over to lie on her stomach beside him. "Why did you buy this house—for real?" His head was resting on his outstretched arm. While she waited for an answer, she combed her fingers through the tangle of his dark blond hair, brushing it back from his temple, where there was a tiny dot of a mole. She yearned to kiss it, but held back.

He answered at last. "I told myself it was a tangible recognition of my success. In the world I grew up in, owning a place in the Hamptons meant you'd made it." His lips twitched self-mockingly. "Now I understand that I also wanted to prove to DeWitt that I wasn't penniless, as he claimed I'd be if I was foolish enough to make writing my career."

"You never did tell me how you became a journalist."

"I was traveling in Europe, scratching for ways to make ends meet, when I came across Harry Bass during his foreign correspondent days. I started doing research for him, and eventually he encouraged me to go back to school for a degree."

"I wonder..." Amalie stroked her knuckles across his cheekbone, remembering something that had struck her when DeWitt Parish had walked in on them at the party.

Jericho turned his head to nibble on her fingers.

"You wonder a lot, don't you?" he said, and nipped at her thumb.

She smiled and rubbed her fingertips over the sand-paper texture of his beard. "I was wondering if you've ever noticed the conspicuous physical similarity between Harry and your stepfather."

Jericho's eyes went opaque. "I suppose you're implying that I latched on to Harry because I was looking for approval from a father figure."

"Well…"

"Maybe you're right. Intellectually."

She laid her head on his chest, the silk of his shirt slippery beneath her cheek. "And emotionally?"

"I prefer not to deal with emotions. They muck up the facts."

She sat up. "That is an incredibly stupid thing to say. *Of course* you deal with emotions. Everyone does."

"In my writing I deal with facts. Emotional perceptions generally cloud the issue, whether they're mine or a subject's. The challenge is to discover the truth that lies behind the facade each person erects to suit their image or the twinges of a guilty conscience."

Amalie slapped the stone hearth. "And *you've* erected a facade made of stone ten feet thick. I can't seem to break through."

"But you have." He propped his head on his hand. "You wormed your way through the cracks, Amalie. You sneaked up on me when I wasn't looking and now you're in every part of me." Again his lips twitched—mocking himself or withholding a smile, she wasn't sure which. "Stone by stone by stone, I've looked," he said. "And you're there."

"Sounds like I'm a creeping fungus or a clinging vine." Sarcasm was the last restraint on her expanding heart.

"No, you're a clematis vine, strong for all its fragility." Clasping her hands, he drew her down to him, his focus her soft rosy lips. "Full of pink flowers good enough to eat."

His kiss was at first a tantalizing promise. Delicate threads of desire floated across her nerve endings. Her lips parted to the probing of his tongue and he deepened the kiss with artful extravagance until she was bound in the sweet, sticky spiderweb of passion, her entire body humming with wanton possibilities.

She measured the thump of his heart beneath her palm. "No emotion, huh?" she said, lightly taunting.

"Well, there's emotion, and then there's sex."

"Sex," she said levelly.

"Madame X would approve."

"Madame X can go fly a kite." Amalie unwound his arm from around her shoulders and climbed on top of him, straddling him with her thighs. She pushed his arms flat and held them down by the wrists, staring into his handsome face. "My name is Amalie Jane Dove and I'm going to teach Thomas Janes Jericho how to make love."

Playfully he struggled against her. "You're going to have to let go to take your clothes off," he warned.

The fire snapped. Amalie did let go, though she remained sitting stolidly over his midriff. Her hand sliced down the placket of his shirt, popping buttons as it went. "Lesson number one. It's *your* clothes that are going to be removed, mister." She discarded her jacket and rolled up her sleeves in preparation.

"First, the shirt. I've seen enough of your white shirts to last me a lifetime." Efficiently she undid the remaining buttons and pulled the tails free, then peeled back the creamy silk to reveal his broad, muscular chest. She swallowed dryly. He was beautiful, utterly virile, sculpted with golden light and dancing shadows from the fireplace. Here was the embodiment of her fantasies, she thought as desire laced her veins. Still, she shouldn't be so easily distracted by a spectacular display of male flesh when there was a job to be done and a lesson to be taught.

Jericho lay compliantly as she skinned the sleeves down his arms with a minimum of maneuvering. He did go up on his elbows when she crawled farther down his legs, her skirt riding up over her thighs. The snap of his jeans was easy, but she frowned in concentration over his zipper, sliding it carefully over the ridge of his growing erection.

She had to stand to tug off the jeans. "Too snug," she said, lifting his feet in turn to do away with his boots and socks.

"They weren't too snug a few minutes ago," he retorted. He laid his head on the blanket and covered his eyes, finding it better not to watch as Amalie ministered to him so solemnly.

She slipped off her own shoes and nylons and knelt beside him. His legs were long and lightly tanned, covered with little, curling brown hairs. Slowly brushing her palms over the rounded muscles of his thighs, she took her time savoring the warm velvety feel of his skin, intrinsically aware of the power and vitality that pulsed just beneath its surface. When he bent one of his knees, she slipped her hand ticklishly along the inside his thigh, making his muscles tense and his skin twitch.

He thunked his head against the floor. "Enough with the preliminaries, Amalie. Let's get to it."

She chuckled. "Lesson number two. Making love properly takes lots of time. Lots and lots of time."

Peering at her beneath the visor of his hands, he said,

"I could throw you down and have you naked in five seconds flat."

She took a page from Lacey's book and batted her lashes coquettishly. "But don't you want to know what I'll remove next?" They both looked at his white briefs, the only thing he was wearing. "And how I'll go about it?" she added with a catlike lick of her lips.

He groaned. "I can last maybe five more minutes."

"We'll see about that," she said, and inched her hands under the elastic waistband. *So hot*, she thought in amazement. What *did* he have in there? Stretching the white cotton, her fingers sought the bulge that was apparently the source of such heat. It stirred, swelling larger. *I've landed a live one*, she thought absurdly, and unsuccessfully tried to smother her laugh.

"What are you doing?" Jericho demanded. He jack-knifed to a sitting position and peeled out of his underwear in the blink of Amalie's eyes, going so far as to toss the offending garment onto the fire, which smoked excessively.

Amalie pressed her lips into a thin line, unaware that her eyes were sparkling like gemstones. "You're a very bad student, throwing your Jockeys in the fire." She ticked his chin with her forefinger. "Lie back now. Let me proceed with the lesson."

Jericho collapsed with another frustrated groan.

Unbridled lust coursed through Amalie when she looked down. Bathed by the flickering light from the fireplace, his erection had a primal beauty, like some sort of ancient fertility symbol. Tentatively she traced its underside with one fingertip. The third lesson was her own, she decided. *Be bold. Be wicked.*

Jericho stopped her when she lowered her head. "Another time," he said, breathing raggedly. "I can't wait—I need to be inside you now."

Her hand closed around his rigid, swollen length. How badly he wanted her! She was struck with the extent of her feminine powers for the first time. One day she would use this knowledge with agonizing skill during their erotic play, but for now the throbbing heat between her own thighs was too insistent to ignore. She was as ready and impatient as he.

"The lessons—" she protested, even as she stripped off her panties and lifted her leg to settle over his supine body, her skirt bunched across her hips. His engorged flesh insinuated itself along her crevice.

"This schoolteacher fantasy of yours takes too long." Jericho's hands fastened on her waist; she rose at their direction.

"No fantasies," she promised, leaning forward slightly with the fingers of one hand splayed across the slick contours of his chest, the cost of his tenuous control being a fine sheen of perspiration. "Just you and me."

With trembling fingers she guided his arousal so the blunt tip was poised at her entrance. Thighs tensed, she paused for a long moment as anticipation gilded her senses, then slowly sank until his distended, thrusting shaft was entirely enveloped. A carnal moan flew uninhibited from her mouth in response to the thrill of being so licentiously filled.

Her hips rocked in a sensuous rhythm; her eyes rolled behind downcast lids. "Mmm, is this why you brought me here?" she asked in dulcet tones.

He grunted. She could feel his buttocks clenching and unclenching. "I brought you here to see the house."

"Why?" She slid up his gleaming length, then down.

"To see if you'd like to live here."

Amalie hesitated at the apex of another upstroke.

Jericho tightened his grip on her waist and rammed her back down as his hips rose with equal force. Her answering "Yes!" came with an exalted gasp as she was showered by vivid fireworks of sensation. Sparks of sizzling pleasure rained down over her skin.

He thrust up into her again and again, establishing a hard, steady rhythm. She threw back her head and rode him wildly. The glittering fireworks intensified and doubled, then redoubled, until the tinder point was reached and she went up in flames of hot convulsing ecstasy.

Still Jericho was hard inside her. Out of breath, she slumped forward, having barely enough strength to hold herself upright. He murmured a question, his hands lowering to her hips to help them grind in unison with his own.

"No, it's all right," she panted. "Keep going." Apparently she wasn't yet satiated. The solid gratification of having him inside her was riveting; her hot-blooded desire renewed itself.

She came alive, her sheer joy spilling over into laughter. In one wrenching motion she stripped off her blouse and bra, flaunting herself just out of Jericho's reach. She was riding high, reveling in a passion that surely was too strong not to have been founded on their mutual love. Even if Jericho wouldn't yet admit it.

"C'mere," he said, and she twined her fingers through his, bending down to reach his lips. Instead of a kiss he executed a wrestling move on her—suddenly she found herself flat on the floor as he'd earlier threatened, with a large, demanding man between her open thighs, sheathing himself inside her, obviously bent on extracting his erotic revenge by method of ravishment. "Told you so," he gloated, and his smile was wicked.

"Ohhh," she sighed sweetly, hiding her own smile,

so pleased with the both of them that she missed the descent of his hand. "Oh," she gasped, sharply inhaling at the blazingly intimate caress of his fingertip. "Oh—oh, Jericho!" she managed to blurt in the midst of the flurry of intoxicating sensations.

His green-gold eyes were incandescent. "I want to see your face this time. I want to watch you come."

And he thrust so deep she felt his presence in every cell of her body. As if his words had released it, another lavish climax took hold at once. And no matter her position, she soared with bliss. Inside and out.

Jericho's mouth claimed Amalie's in hot obsession as his own coursing climax arrived. She threaded her fingers through his hair to hold him fast, her kisses so loving and generous his heart contracted. With a great gusting sigh he collapsed beside her, pulling her into his arms so their contact was not broken for an instant. He didn't ask himself why, he simply held her close as they shuddered through the languorous aftershocks.

The fire had died down to red glowing embers. The high-ceilinged room would soon grow cold, but for now they were warm with exertion. Jericho stroked the soft swell of Amalie's stomach, brushing his fingertips from hipbone to hipbone and idly wondering how a baby fit in a space so small and then more sharply asking himself why he was thinking of *that*. Amalie distracted him by turning to press herself against him. With a small purring sound, she wound her arms around his neck and tucked her head into the hollow of his shoulder. Her lips moved against his skin.

He waited for her to speak. She did not.

"Did you mean it?" he asked at last, having to tear the words loose from his formidable reserve. "Could you live here with me?"

Her slender shoulders shivered. "I don't

know...maybe." He caressed her nape, the wispy ends of her dark hair tickling the back of his hand. "It depends," she added.

His hand stilled. "On what?"

"On what the offer entails."

"Do you mean a marriage certificate?" He pulled back slightly, but her face was still hidden, so he kept talking even though he had no control over what he was saying. "I can probably give you that."

She rolled onto her back and drew her thighs up to her chest. "Logically. Intellectually. Unemotionally," she said in a singsong voice, tapping her knees lightly with her fists. Her gaze slanted toward him. "Tell me, Jericho, what you think we just did."

He knew what she wanted him to say, he just wasn't sure that saying it would be honest. "We..." He cleared his throat and said it anyway. "We made love."

She sighed and sat up, turning her back on him. "I wish I could believe you meant that." Reaching for her clothes, she surreptitiously swiped the back of one wrist across her eyes.

"I don't lie," he said. Some unexamined impulse made him sit up and pull her roughly into his arms, folding his legs around hers, hugging her to his chest, using his body to cradle hers in warmth and comfort.

"Then answer me this—honestly," she challenged him almost belligerently.

His chin rested on the top of her head. "I'll try."

"Can you really be happy in this house, with or without me?"

Jericho tried to concentrate, but his gaze returned to the windows that faced the Parish house even though he could see nothing beyond the black night and a ghostly image of their pale, naked bodies reflected in the glass. The house meant nothing to him, he realized. Not even as a status symbol—which was the very thing he'd sworn to despise.

"Happiness isn't what I was thinking about when I bought it," he said to Amalie. "One house does just as well as another, I suppose. I have to live somewhere."

"You're wrong," she said softly, but didn't elaborate. "Another question," she continued after a few moments. "Why do you withhold your emotions, not just from me, but from everyone? Your friends, your parents...yourself?"

He felt the familiar icy control taking over. "I told you, Amalie. I don't bother with emotions."

She twisted around to slap at his chest. "Liar!" She hit him again, pushing ineffectually at solid muscle, her expression fierce. "You made love to me, Jericho, I know you did. I felt it!"

"But that's—"

"It's not just sex!" She grabbed him by the nape and kissed him hard, her teeth clashing against his, her tongue stabbing into his mouth. He put his hands to the back of her head to gentle her. A tear slid down the slope of her cheek into his mouth and he tasted pain, desire, doubt, deep affection.

Emotion.

Amalie tore her mouth from his. "Either I truly am the most naive person on the face of the earth or you're the stubbornest, Jericho, because I refuse to believe that you cannot feel love." She brushed his hands away and stood, a slight figure in tones of cream and pink and black velvet, her eyes a blazing electric blue.

"The truth is that I would love to be your wife."

He closed his eyes, concentrating on the wonderfully

strange, messy and illogical feelings that were taking unwieldy control of his heart.

Amalie continued. "But I can't say yes until you know why you'd want me to be."

And Thomas Janes Jericho opened his eyes. At last.

12

Swept away by the glorious rush of sensation, she rolled her head in the gray sand, soft bleating sounds the least insensible of all that she uttered....

"Miss Starling?"

Amy Lee opened her eyes to the sight of the school principal's elderly, needle-nosed secretary exuding weaselly concern. "Miss Starling, are you ill?" the secretary asked. "You appear to have a fever."

"I'll be fine after I open a window." Flustered to be caught in the midst of an after-school daydream, Amy Lee made a show of fanning her pink cheeks. "It's rather hot for September, isn't it? A shame we all had to spend the day in the classroom."

The secretary was dubious. "Once you've pulled yourself together perhaps you'd care to report to Mr. Smith's office. He asked to see you before you left for the day."

Demurely Amy Lee lowered her lashes. "I'll go at once."

AMALIE WAS NOT PREPARED for what she encountered on her return trip to Belle Isle. Although Bookcon had buzzed about her sudden prominence as author of the *Black Velvet* books, and she'd been approached by several journalists eager for the inside scoop, she hadn't expected word to have reached the island so soon. Jericho's *NewsProfile* article would be published in several days; she'd intended to use the grace period to find a way to explain matters to her parents.

Apparently the news had leaked beyond literary circles.

The gulls flapping and squawking around the pier did not sound unlike the knot of reporters and camera people gathered around Chick Garrity, the jack-of-all-trades harbor operator. Amalie slung her tote bag over her shoulder and departed the midmorning ferry with a half-dozen other passengers, keeping her profile low as she strode past the garrulous gathering. Chick, looking confused by the onslaught, raised his hands to quiet the reporters. "One at a time, folks. I can't make out head nor tails."

"Do you know Senator Dove's daughter, Amalie?" someone squawked, leveling a microphone at Chick's homely face.

Amalie's step faltered as she darted a quick glance over her shoulder. *Of course.* Someone, somewhere, had connected her to the senator from South Carolina, a senator whose role in the antipornography hearings a couple years past had been prominent enough that her relationship to the erstwhile Madame X was national news.

Fortunately, Chick didn't point her out to the reporters. Maybe he hadn't seen her? "Sure I know Amalie Dove," he said jovially. "This is a small island. I know everybody."

The members of the media clamored. The voice of a blond woman wearing a designer suit and tennis shoes rose shrilly. "Can you give us directions to her house?"

Please don't do it, Chick, Amalie silently pleaded as

she stepped up her getaway. The tearoom waited halfway down Harbor Street. If she could reach it, she could duck inside and call Marydoe or John for a ride home. And if her luck held from there, her parents would be back from D.C. and she could spill her guts before the reporters descended.

While Amalie trotted along the sidewalk, Chick rubbed his grizzled chin. ''Well, now, first you go that way,'' he said, pointing in the direction opposite from Beaufort Road. ''Till you run into the fork in the road. Then you'll want to turn right and drive near a mile to Loggerhead Point….''

He was directing them southeast, deep into the wildest part of the island, Amalie realized gratefully. They could even get lost out there, and with houses few and far between, there'd be nobody to ask for directions. *Thank you, Chick.* She hitched up the strap of her tote and kicked open the tearoom's Victorian spindle screen door.

What Una Bray insisted on calling a tearoom was actually a restaurant made up of an off-the-wall juxtaposition of Victorian furnishings laced with antimacassars, beaded lamp shades, flocked wallpaper, tacky tourist merchandise and a fifties-era counter and stools. Luckily for Una, her home-baked, down-home food was good enough to make up for the decor.

Oddly, no one in the tearoom greeted Amalie when she stepped inside, even though she could tell by their eyes that they'd registered her arrival. The hope planted by Chick's favor wilted in the heavy, unnatural silence. Clearly, word about her Madame X secret had already spread through town. Had they all decided that Amalie Dove, a.k.a. Madame X, was an embarrassment to Belle Isle? Were they ashamed to acknowledge her?

"Hey, Nellie," said Ruby Riley, the redheaded waitress who'd been Amalie's childhood friend. She waved in a friendly manner from behind the counter.

Amalie looked over her shoulder.

"Have a nice shopping trip to the mainland, *Nellie?*" Ruby asked, staring straight at Amalie. "Why don't you have a seat? Can I get you a cup of coffee, *Nellie?*"

Amalie plopped onto one of the red leatherette stools. "Why are you—"

Ruby interrupted. "You'd rather have a cold drink, I bet." She was making faces now, rolling her eyes like marbles, ponytail whipping to and fro as her head twitched like a dog with fleas.

Knowing something was wrong, but not remotely what, Amalie held herself still as her gaze slid along the row of customers seated at the counter. Mike Nestor's round face was as red as a boiled lobster; he hunched over a cup of coffee, his downcast eyes glued to the doughnut he'd mechanically dunked so many times it was a glob of soggy mush. Mike was a shy, middle-aged bachelor, so she couldn't really blame him for finding the Madame X erotica embarrassing, but why was even Clint, the town's self-avowed, up-for-anything playboy, doing his best not to notice her? Why, Clint should've been goggle-eyed over her books! She wouldn't have been surprised to find him standing on the rungs of his bar stool, reading select passages aloud.

Then Amalie noticed the man seated beside Clint. She didn't know his name, but she recognized him from a mainland six-o'clock news program. In between scribbling on a clipboard, he was sipping Una's secret-recipe iced tea and keeping his eye on the street in case the pack of reporters kicked up any interesting developments in the hunt for Amalie Dove. He nudged

Clint's elbow. "This Madame X must be one hot number, I bet. You positive you don't know her? Maybe you went to high school with her?"

"Amalie left the island to attend school," Ruby said, aggressively wiping the counter clean with a rag. She whisked away the reporter's glass even though it was only half-empty. "I don't know where, so don't ask me."

The TV reporter looked up and saw Amalie watching him. "What about you, miss? Do you know Amalie Dove?"

Her attempt at a smile skittered across her face like a water bug on the surface of a pond. "M-my name's Nellie."

The reporter took this as an invitation. "Live on the island, do you, Nellie?" he said, coming over to sit beside her. He was young and handsome in a clean-cut way, with a habit of looking around and smoothing his hair as if cameras were always in the vicinity. "I hear the Doves own most of the island, so it's kind of surprising that so few of you seem to know anything about the family."

"They keep to themselves," she murmured.

"Hoity-toity?" he asked sharply. "Big-deal senator and doctor, am I right? Old Southern family?" He glanced around again and stroked his sideburns. "I see they got their name on the library and museum and who knows what all. Townsfolk might resent that."

"Young man, that's no way to talk about the Doves!" Una Bray, five feet tall and three feet wide, wild gray hair crackling about her head, came out of the kitchen wielding a greasy spatula. As usual, she'd been imbibing on the cooking sherry, so she'd missed most of the conversation. She looked at Amalie and lifted her lip in disgust. "Your daddy's a fine man. I would think you'd stand up—"

Ruby screamed like a banshee and pointed into the kitchen. "Smoke! Fire!"

"What?" said the reporter.

There *was* smoke billowing out of the kitchen. Clint kneeled on his bar stool and craned his neck to see into the kitchen. "That's no fire, that's Una's bacon drippings."

Ruby lashed him with a dish towel. "Heck, Nellie, I hope you don't report us for this," she said loudly as she shoved Una back into the kitchen.

The man from the TV station was rightfully confused. "Wait a minute." He looked at Amalie with suspicion. "Didn't that cook say—"

"C'mon, Nellie." Behind the reporter's back, Ruby squinched her eyes and pointed her thumb toward the back room, where Una and her four fishermen brothers played poker on Saturday nights. When the reporter swiveled around, Ruby dropped her hand and smiled blandly. "Nellie's the health inspector."

Mike's doughnut had fallen into his coffee. "A mean one," he improvised bashfully.

"Whoo, the tearoom's in for it now," Ruby said, coming around the counter to take Amalie by the elbow. "Let me show you the bathrooms. I'm afraid they're in quite a state!"

"A whole other state would do me fine," Amalie said as soon as they were out of the reporter's hearing. "Thanks for getting me out of there."

Ruby put her hands on her ample hips. "Why didn't you *tell* me, Amalie? I thought we were friends!"

Amalie had to admit that Ruby, with her so-what attitude, easy way with men and consequently shady reputation, would probably be the last one to criticize

Amalie's new occupation. "I don't know, Ruby. I guess I was too shy."

The waitress smacked her forehead. "Too shy? Those books! I couldn't rightly believe it when people started saying *you* wrote them. They're so steamy!" Playfully she wiped imaginary sweat from her brow.

Amalie had to smile. "And I'm so…"

"You're so well behaved." Ruby looked Amalie up and down and shook her head. The waitress wasn't a conventional beauty, but she was robust, buxom and oozing with cheerful sexuality. Men, on the whole, were suitably engaged by her bountiful charms—some in town said too often for decorum's sake.

"Come to think of it, though, I do remember a time when you were nearly as much a hellion as me." Ruby chuckled. "Way back when."

"Before I went away to school."

"Yeah." Ruby nodded eagerly. "When you came back you were so proper that me and Mose and Charlie didn't recognize you. I was about fourteen then, and growing these hips and boobs…." She gestured at her hourglass shape. "Your new clothes and sophisticated ways intimidated me."

"I never realized you felt that way. You called me stuck-up."

"Did I?" Ruby shrugged. "Probably. I was pretty defensive back then—self-conscious about my, let's say, *humble* roots." She laughed loudly, with a lingering trace of defiance. "And that's the nicest way anyone's ever put it."

Now that she'd met Jericho, Amalie better understood how Ruby might feel about her less-than-ideal family circumstances. She smiled tentatively. "Well, now that we're—"

"Hey!" the TV reporter shouted from the tearoom.

"Hey! Nellie's no health inspector! You said she was on a shopping trip!" Sounds of a tussle ensued.

Ruby peeked past the tattered velvet curtain that did for a door. "Amalie, you better get out of here quick. Use the back door."

"Thanks." She slipped through the room crowded with more shabby Victorian furnishings, then paused with her hand on the latch to the back exit. "Do you think I can make it to my house?"

"The island's crawling with reporters," Ruby said dubiously as she headed into the tearoom to reinforce Mike and Clint's defense. "Good luck!"

The alley was deserted. Grateful that her photograph wasn't yet plastered over the wire services, at least, Amalie quickly made her way to the southern end of Harbor Street. Although she didn't dare try walking out to Beaufort Drive and risk being set upon by a pack of reporters, perhaps she could hitch a ride.

Warily, she edged around the post office building. From what she could see, most of the reporters had left the pier area to follow Chick's wayward directions out to Loggerhead Point, giving her maybe twenty or thirty minutes to reach her parents.

A car was cruising down the road at ten miles per hour, sunshine glancing off its windshield. Amalie stepped off the curb to wave it down. The Crawford sisters were the only ones she knew who, in their shiny new Cadillac, tooled around town slower than the speed limit. They lived in the perfectly kept, wedding-cake antebellum mansion at 8 Belleport Drive, so if they were heading home they might give her a ride.

Apparently not. When the Caddy came within spitting distance—certainly close enough for the sisters to recognize Amalie—it suddenly veered off, bumping over the opposite curb and through the intersection at double its previous speed. Amalie was left in the street with her hand hovering in the air.

She dropped it. "I've been snubbed," she said aloud, curious about her reaction. There was little. Chick's, Mike's, Ruby's and even Clint's helpful concern counted for more than Alberta Crawford's aghast, handkerchief-pressed-to-the-mouth avoidance.

"Hey!" someone shouted. "Hey, you!"

Amalie looked up to see that the TV reporter had emerged from the tearoom and was hailing her. Instinctively, she turned on her heel and raced up the hill toward the renovated tabby buildings that housed the Jessup P. Dove Memorial Library, Museum and Archives. The incline was long and steep. The heavy tote bag bumped against her hip as she ran as fast as she used to when Blackbeard's ghost was on her tail.

"Are you Amalie Dove?" the reporter called, loping after her. "The author of *Black Velvet?*"

Lungs straining, she crashed pell-mell through a clump of pink flowering azaleas, threw her bag onto the veranda and hauled herself up over the railing. Her key ring had sifted down to the bottom of the bag; she tossed clothing out indiscriminately, scrabbled through the keys and inserted the proper one into the lock of the tall double doors. The disheveled reporter charged up the veranda steps, shouting questions as Amalie shoveled up her belongings, grabbed the keys, stepped inside and slammed the door in his face.

He shaded his eyes to peer through the etched glass inset. "Amalie Dove? Madame X? How do you justify profiting from sexually explicit literature when your own mother campaigned against pornography?"

Amalie backed away, almost tripping over her deflated tote bag and scattered possessions. Righting herself with the help of the newel post of the stairway, she glanced around the foyer which separated the museum from the library. It was dark with the museum shutters closed for the off-season, but she knew the space as well as her own home. She trotted up the stairway to her office on the second floor, leaving the TV reporter futilely calling her name.

How *could* she justify herself to her mother? Amalie's hand shook as she unlocked the small office from which she ran both the library and the museum, with the aid of volunteers from the Belle Isle Historical Society. Saying that she'd intended to remain anonymous just didn't cut it.

Breathing hard, she sat at her desk with her head in her hands for a long minute, then picked up the phone and dialed. Answering machine. "Jericho? Hi, it's Amalie. I'm home on Belle Isle, where are you? Wish you were here...." She chuckled, then groaned. "No, maybe I don't. I'm stuck in my office above the library—there's a pack of reporters nipping at my heels. Literally. I need..." *You*, she almost blurted, but bit her lip instead, and while she was trying to figure out how she could say "I love you" without scaring him off, the machine beeped.

Jericho had expressed surprise that she wasn't holding a grudge about his article exposing her as Madame X. Amalie was a little surprised herself. She'd meant to be angry at him, but somewhere between here and there she'd realized that he was only doing his job. She couldn't blame him when all he'd done was what she may have subconsciously been wanting but was too timid to do for herself.

True, there were plenty of drawbacks to the situation, and, as illustrated by her precipitous journey up the hill, she wasn't sure how to handle them. She did know that it had felt good to take the author's chair in

Pebblepond's Bookcon booth. Scary and intimidating, too, but mainly good.

Facing the press was another matter. And facing her parents...

"Coward," she said, and picked up the phone.

Her father, James Jessup Dove, answered.

"Dad, it's me," she whispered, her hand cupped over the receiver as if someone was listening in. "Amalie."

"Amalie—where are you?"

"Home. I mean, on Belle Isle, but I couldn't make it all the way home. I'm in my office at the library."

"You know about the reporters, then."

Was that censure in his voice? Amalie wasn't certain. Her father was a doctor, a general practitioner who'd started a health service for the low-income inhabitants of the scattered Sea Islands. When his wife, who'd been politically active throughout their marriage, was ultimately elected to the senate, he'd taken early retirement so he could move with her to Washington. Proud of his family's long and illustrious history, he'd always told Amalie that whatever she did, she must live up to the Dove name.

"I'm sorry, Dad." Nervously she wound the phone cord around her wrist. "I know I should have told you—"

"Hold on, Amalie. Your mother just got off the other line. She wants to speak to you."

Amalie's pulse picked up again.

Barbara Dove's cultured voice came on the line. "Madame X, I presume?"

Oh, boy. Amalie's voice quavered. "Mo-om?"

"Amalie Jane Dove, you sound just like you used to when you and your rowdy friends got into another bad patch of mischief. Do you remember what I'd say to you?"

"You'd say that as long as I hadn't done something that was irreparably harmful, you wouldn't have to punish me. Then you'd make me repair the damage, or work it off, or at least apologize." Amalie swallowed. "I don't think that tactic is going to work this time."

"Have you done something irreparably harmful?"

"Probably. I might have even cost you the next election."

"Not likely, dear. In only a few months this little contretemps of yours will be forgotten. I'm not up for reelection for another two years."

Little contretemps? "It doesn't feel little to me, Mom."

"I suppose not." Barbara sighed regretfully. "You really should have told your father and me what you were up to. I can't quite believe my daughter became a bestselling author and I didn't even know it when I read—"

Amalie interrupted. "Don't tell me you've read one of the books."

"Well…" Her mother chuckled. "Your father brought home a copy of *Black Velvet* this past Valentine's Day—oh, now, Jim, don't be making faces at me. It's time this family opened a dialogue, I must say."

Amalie made a sound of shocked mortification.

"Anyway, Amalie, little did we know… Goodness, your father's beginning to blush. I suppose I shouldn't go into details."

"I think I have to go now, Mom."

"Should we come and pick you up?"

"No! I'll work something out. I don't want to face the press just yet, and they'll only get worse if you show up. Uh, is there anything I can say, some statement or other, to help you out? Politically, I mean?"

"That's generous of you to offer, but I do think you've done more than enough. My staff is in an uproar." Barbara laughed. "Don't worry, dear. They're working on the proper politically correct statement to release to the media. If I have to I'll hold a brief press conference. This will all blow over, you'll see."

"Not soon enough for me," Amalie muttered after they'd said their goodbyes and hung up. But she did feel relieved. They'd gotten past the initial awkwardness, and by the time they came face-to-face they'd all have had time to adjust. Still, the thought of her father going out and *buying* the book was just—!

Amalie snatched up the phone and pressed out Jericho's number before she could question the advisability of her impulse. "Me, again," she said to his answering machine. "Listen, what I actually wanted to say is...I love you, Jericho." She hesitated. "That's all, really."

That's everything.

EARLIER THAT SAME MORNING, Jericho was in Harry Bass's Manhattan office. As editor-in-chief of *NewsProfile*, Harry was entitled to an expansive, plush, corporate space. He'd turned it into a jumble. Hiding somewhere beneath stacks of papers, folders and magazines, behind rows and rows of videotapes, books and fat binders of vital information, and under a flurry of memos, stick-on notes and crumpled balls of paper, was a hand-woven wool rug, matching teak bookcases and desk, and a state-of-the-art computer. One just couldn't see them.

Jericho cleared a chair and sat near Harry's desk with a cup of black coffee. He counted six assorted in-progress coffees on Harry's desk and coffee table, everything from ice-cold dregs in a ceramic mug to a steaming plastic cup.

Harry looked up from the layout of the Madame X article he'd been perusing. "I'm not changing a thing."

"We've got to. The story's changed, Harry. Word is out."

"We'll still be the first national newsmagazine to print it." Harry waved a mock-up of the cover. "*And* we've got exclusive photos of the fake Madame X side by side with the real one."

Jericho winced. It wasn't that the shadowy photo of a moody-looking Amalie was bad as much as it was the contrast between it and the glossy glamour shot of Lacey. The headline in lurid red—The Two Sides of Madame X—didn't help. "At least take my name off the cover," he said.

Harry was disbelieving. "You're giving up a cover byline?"

"I think it's best…considering my involvement."

Harry guffawed. "Company policy dictates a reprimand, but I gotta congratulate you first, Jericho. What a swordsman!"

"It wasn't like that," Jericho said uncomfortably.

Harry gulped from the plastic cup, his eyes narrowing behind the rising steam. "Don't tell me…"

Jericho grimaced. It was the only way he could keep the big, goofy grin off his face.

"You're not…" Harry couldn't say the dreaded words. "Don't do it, Jericho. Women are an anathema. I know they look all soft and willing, but that's just for the first few months. After that, marriage is sheer hell. The divorce is worse."

"I take it Rosie's still mad about you messing with her bestseller."

Harry huffed. "At least she's talking to me." When he saw Jericho's grin, he added hastily, "And it's torture." He made the sign of the cross. "Ward 'em off, Jericho. You're our last holdout. Don't succumb. Hell, she's probably not even a real blonde."

Jericho stared at the cup he was passing from hand to hand. "It's not actually the blonde I, er..."

Startled, Harry grabbed up the cover to examine it again. "This is bad. Really bad. Not a good sign at all." When Jericho started to speak, Harry waved him off. "Do you mean to tell me that you had a choice of these two women and you went for the dark-haired, flat-chested, skinny one?"

"She has a name, Harry, not just a body."

"Oh, this is bad," the editor groaned. "Reminds me of how I ended up with Rosie."

"Who was—is—the love of your life, by the way?"

Harry plunged his hands into his curly white hair. "Yeah. The love of my life."

"You and Rosie had eighteen great years together. You could probably have eighteen more if you'd stop acting like such an idiot."

"Since when did you turn into Ann Landers? You're the man with a heart of stone."

"Not anymore, Harry," Jericho admitted. And this time he couldn't stop the big, goofy smile from making an appearance.

The burly editor beamed even as he swore a blue streak. "Then, damn it," he finally concluded, "I guess congratulations are in order. Never thought I'd see the day."

Harry's approval meant more to Jericho than he'd realized. Getting it made him feel damn good—even proud. So Amalie had been right about Harry's father-figure status after all, he concluded, standing to shake the editor's hand, choosing to count himself lucky that he'd found Harry Bass instead of unlucky for also being stuck with DeWitt Parish.

"Don't know if congratulations are called for yet," Jericho said gruffly, emotion clogging his throat, "but thanks just the same."

"Hmm." Harry eyeballed the upcoming *NewsProfile* cover. "You're in hot water about this?"

"Just like you with Rosie."

"Women." Harry grunted. "They don't know how to keep business separate."

Jericho could no longer say that he did, either, not after Amalie had smashed his vaunted objectivity to smithereens.

"Then you'd better go persuade her to see it your way," Harry groused, "because I'm not about to change a word in this story just because you've got the hots for Madame X. No matter which one of 'em you chose."

"Thanks for the advice, Ann." Grinning, Jericho walked quickly to the door. He had a plane to catch, but he took the time to add as he left, "Take your own advice, why don't you, Harry? Rosie's probably waiting for you to make the first move."

Harry Bass stared at the framed picture of his ex-wife that was the only personal item in the cluttered office. "Love," he growled. "It gets us all in the end."

13

Under the secretary's watchful eye, Amy Lee paused outside the principal's office door, wondering if she was presentable. She smoothed her straight dark hair back into its bun and bloused the front of her shirt, trying to camouflage the pouter-pigeon plumpness of her figure. Fortunately, not even the suspicious secretary who'd walked in on the end of her fantasy would ever imagine that the meek schoolteacher Amy Lee Starling engaged in such a variety of amorous activities.

Amy Lee knocked. "Come in," said Mr. Smith, the new principal she'd not met formally until the first day of school. She entered, careful to close and silently lock the door behind her.

Mr. Smith approached her as he had that first night on the beach, as he had when they'd trysted there throughout the remainder of a summer so ripe and rich with sensuality she'd wished for it to never end. And, in a way, it hadn't.

His eyes radiated the same sexual heat even now that they'd been introduced. "My secretary is concerned about your state of mind, Miss Starling. She said your behavior is suspect."

"It is indeed, Mr. Smith." A naughty thrill teased Amy Lee's lips into a smile. "Why, I've been positively wicked."

AMALIE SPENT THE REST of the morning and afternoon holed up in her office. Every now and then she peeked out the window to see if the TV reporter was still there, and he was, joined first by his cameraman and then by a straggling group of those of his comrades intrepid enough to stick around after Chick's wild-goose chase had run them ragged. From what Amalie could tell from her second-story vantage point, the islanders were going about business as usual, stopping by the tearoom, bait shop or post office while keeping a wary eye on the reporters. Very few seemed inclined to give interviews.

Lunching on corn chips and soda from the vending machines, Amalie hatched a plan for her escape. She called Ruby at the tearoom, who called her sister, Maggie, because Maggie was short and skinny and owned more wigs than Dolly Parton. Next Amalie called the Belle Isle Community Airport to ask a favor of her other childhood friend, Charlie. Then she called Ruby back. Once they'd coordinated the logistics, she called home and found out that her mother was arranging a five o'clock press conference at the pier, which would work perfectly as a further distraction. Amalie explained about Jericho's article, and what she was up to, then requested a getaway car.

And after all that, she had nothing to do but sit and worry. She flipped through a few days' worth of mail, found she couldn't concentrate worth beans and went to stand by the window again. The reporters were sprawled on the steps leading up to the veranda, looking hot and bored. Served them right.

She took a turn around the second floor to stretch her legs. The vending machines had been installed in the large meeting room used by various island groups, but she was sick of snack food. A warren of rooms at the back of the building served as storage for the bulk of the archives not on display downstairs in the museum. As curator and archivist, Amalie had solicited interesting items from most of the old island families, including her own. The Dove family archives were so vast she'd yet to reach their limit. Whenever she finished identifying, cataloging and preserving one lot, Marydoe pulled another trunk or cardboard box out of the attic.

The boxful Amalie was currently working on contained a hodgepodge—everything from fading photos of Jessup P. Dove on a 1902 safari to the feminine ephemera of a long-forgotten aunt. Hoping to find something to occupy herself until Ruby and Maggie arrived, Amalie plucked out a thin, cloth-covered diary. She'd glanced through it only cursorily up to now.

She returned to sit at her desk. The diary was faded and fragile, signed by Prudence Farley Dove, a spinster who'd summered on the island back when it was still called Lone Belle Isle some two hundred years ago, if Amalie was remembering her family tree and history correctly. She sighed and put up her feet. Island history usually intrigued her, but she knew at a glance that this diary was bound to be pretty dry.

And it was, for the most part. But not entirely. When Amalie reached the part about the ship that had anchored in the harbor during a storm, she sat up and took notice. With a delicate yet deft turn of phrase, Prudence Dove had described the captain of the ship as a man so virile her tame virgin heart was set all aflutter—though not in so many words, of course. She seemed to imply that he was suspected of being a smuggler, perhaps even a pirate.

Eagerly Amalie turned the page—to a recipe for trifle, serving twenty-four. "Rats," she said, and skimmed the remainder of the diary, hoping for *something*, some sign of life or romance or illicit rendezvous on a deserted moonlit beach. She found nothing but stitch-by-stitch descriptions of quilting bees and the downright rolicsome tale of a raccoon in the outhouse.

Though she was frustrated enough to heave it across the room, Amalie carefully laid the brittle diary on the desk. Poor Prudence, long gone and apparently unlamented. There'd been scarcely a hint of it in her writings, but Amalie was certain her maiden ancestor had once itched to be wicked. Certainly she'd wished for love and romance and excitement, just like Amalie. Maybe she'd even wanted to run naked on the beach.

Exactly like Amalie.

Who'd never quite dared, even when she was ten and still untamed.

Except in her books—which in the end would count for nothing but another entry in the Dove family archives.

Amalie leaned her chin on her palm. True, she wasn't exactly a stifled spinster, especially since she'd met Jericho. Her journals made for better reading than Prudence's diary, even *before* she'd met Jericho.

And she had finally told him that she loved him, if only on an answering machine.

Yet there was one more leap of faith to make.

She had to go all the way. She had to *dare*.

JERICHO ARRIVED on Belle Isle in a propeller plane that rattled like it was made of tinfoil. Taking the ferry would have been less hair-raising, but he'd suddenly felt that time was of the essence. Amalie had looked brave but vulnerable, biting her bottom lip as she told him that she had to go home to face the oncoming tide of unwelcome publicity. Still uncertain about his brand-new emotions, Jericho had let her go without him, then instantly regretted it even though there'd been a possibility that the best he could do for her was to soften the *NewsProfile* article. The morning's meeting with Harry had made a wash of that plan.

So here Jericho was, the instigator of Amalie's downfall, ready to offer whatever support he could. During the flight south, he'd looked at his family situation with the kind of dispassion he'd once imagined he'd attained, and had seen that there was nothing he could do to make DeWitt Parish the father he'd craved instead of the father whose rejection had twisted him into knots so tight they'd only recently begun to unravel. Seeing how abruptly the Parishes had dismissed Amalie—and with such an extreme prejudice that even she, who was as good as she was bad, didn't have a chance—had cured Jericho of the feeling that their lack of family relationship was his fault. The failing rested mainly with his stepfather. Jericho would no longer accept its burden, and already his heart had grown immeasurably lighter.

The western sky was washed in pale orange as the plane circled Belle Isle, preparing to land at its Podunk airport. The island had hovered in a misty gray-green haze until proximity clarified the perspective, picking out the sharper emerald of the forest, the green-gold swaths of salt marshes and the shiny brown mud flats. Slashes of gray beach were bounded by sapphire water laced with the white spit of the surf. It seemed to Jericho that Amalie lived in paradise.

And his paradise lived in Amalie.

An astounding realization: he was off-his-rocker in love with her.

A warm sweep of air hit him as soon as he left the plane. Near the low-slung airport terminal grew dense clumps of palmettos and thick-scented banana shrubs. A tiny green lizard clung to a louvered window. Jericho grinned.

Once inside, his good cheer did nothing to help him find Amalie. The girl behind the ticket counter was uncommunicative; another airport worker scowled as Jericho requested directions to the Dove's place on Beaufort Drive, and asked if he was a reporter. Jericho couldn't lie even though his mission was strictly personal, so he didn't get help from that source, either. He decided that by the look of the town from the air, it shouldn't be that difficult to find the proper road. After renting a ten-year-old Jeep—the absolute last vehicle available, the girl said; didn't he know they had a bunch of reporters in town?—he crossed toward the exit doors of the nearly deserted terminal.

The doors banged open and a dark-haired pixie darted inside. He put out his hand to stop her. When she looked up he saw that she wasn't Amalie, even though she was wearing a prissy lavender suit similar to the one Amalie had put on again that morning. The look-alike's hair was short and black, but it was also threaded with a shock of red at one temple. Jericho squinted. Was he imagining things or was that a really bad wig?

"Leave go," the girl said, the tiny bell on the gold hoop that pierced her nostril tinkling as she jerked her arm away.

The man who'd scowled at Jericho waved her toward the other door with a ticket in his hand. "The plane takes off in five minutes," he said, then looked at Jericho and scowled again. "Miss Dove," he added in a loud voice.

A relative of Amalie's? Jericho wondered, rooted in place.

A minute later, a group of five or six out-of-breath reporters—he'd know them anywhere—and photographers—the cameras were his first clue—burst into the terminal. "Did you see a short, dark-haired woman?" a cleft-chinned pretty boy shouted as they ran by. Jericho nodded and pointed at the door that opened to the tarmac. Having gotten an inkling of what Amalie had done, he wasted no time in taking off in the opposite direction.

It was about half a mile into town, which as it turned out was larger than it looked from the air, though not by much. When Jericho spotted the gathering at the harbor, he parked nearby and went to check it out just in case.

While there was no podium, glaring lights or thick tangle of microphones, he recognized a press conference when he saw one. Senator Barbara Dove stood at the front of the crowd in one of those solid-color suits female politicians always wore, her puffy dark hair flipping in the ocean breeze. "I am quite proud of my daughter's literary talent," she was saying over the slap of water on the pilings. "Many would-be writers try, but so few can lay claim to bestseller status." Though her charming three-corner smile was just like Amalie's, there was a bit of a bite to the statement. Jericho estimated that many of the journalists present had a half-finished or finished-and-rejected manuscript hidden in one of their desk drawers. Reminding them of that fact wasn't going to curry any favor.

He jumped in with a question. "What are your daughter's current whereabouts, Senator Dove?"

She looked him in the eye for a long moment. "I missed your name."

He tried to appear trustworthy. "Thomas Janes Jericho, *NewsProfile*."

"Ah." Barbara Dove's eyes sparkled. "Well, Mr. Jericho, I'm afraid you've missed all the excitement. Madame X tore out of here not ten minutes ago, heading for the airport. She prefers to retain some semblance of anonymity." The senator shrugged. "We all have our flaws." The reporters chuckled. "Amalie Dove has flown the coop," she continued smoothly. "Or should I say, the *dovecote?*"

Jericho raised his eyebrows. Why did that word ring a bell?

"Let's get back to your antipornography stand, Senator," one of the newspaper reporters said. "Isn't it hypocritical to approve of your daughter's books and yet attack the output of someone like Larry Flynt?"

Senator Dove answered even while she obliquely watched Jericho slip out of the small crowd. "How many ways can I put this? I defend the right to free speech. What I do not accept is the demeaning victimization of women...."

Jericho waved at Amalie's mother as he drove away. She gave no sign she'd noticed, but he knew she had. And he knew she'd given him a clue—if he could just remember what it meant.

The island was shrouded in dusk when he finally found Beaufort Drive after fifteen minutes of aimless meandering. Fortunately, his reporter's memory for detail had kicked in and he'd remembered where he'd heard the name Dovecote.

No longer looking for Amalie's family home, he gunned the Jeep past the oyster-shell driveway of the looming gothic peaks of 12 Beaufort and took the dirt track that led to the beach. Beyond the dunes, the ocean swelled and receded, an endless ribbon of deep indigo blue glistening in the fading light.

First, Jericho checked all the huge live oaks near the

house, walking beneath the festoons of Spanish moss that trailed from their branches. There were no tree houses named Dovecote to be seen. He crested the dune and looked up and down the beach, seeking a hint, a trail, maybe an instinctive whisper of the heart.

Though his heart was filled with hope and longing instead of cold despair, it still didn't speak to him, so Jericho shrugged and listened to his common sense instead. He turned right, away from the lights of the Doves' nearest neighbor. After a minute, he kicked off his shoes and walked barefoot, his toes curling into the cool sand.

Impossible to build an elaborate tree house in the towering sea pines, he decided, and he wasn't eager to walk very deeply into the damp, dark, spongy marshland. He was wondering if islands had alligators when he saw her.

She was standing shin deep in the shallows, wearing a very un-Amalielike, grimy Carolina Panthers tank top and rolled-up jeans, her hands in the back pockets. She didn't see him until he lifted his arm to wave, and then she turned, brushing her hair out of her eyes.

"Amalie!" he called, relishing her name, her true name.

"Jericho!" Her voice sailed on the wind.

He tossed his shoes away and started to run.

THE MOMENT FELT LIKE a dream, but Jericho was so real. He was large and hard and warm and rough and velvet all at once, lifting her high in his arms, kissing her and telling her how much he loved her. *How much he loved her.*

Amalie turned her face up to the sky, wanting to shout with joy. "You got my message!"

She felt his smile against her neck. "Yeah, I finally got the message."

She twined her legs and arms around him and clung like a vine to crumbling stone. "I meant the one I left on your answering machine."

"I haven't been home. I left Harry's office and came straight here." He put his hands under her derriere and strode out of the saltwater to dry sand. "Was the message anything important?"

"Not much. Just that I love you, too." Feeling silly and giggly, she kissed and nipped and nibbled at his jaw, his cheekbone, his earlobe. "Just that I loved you first." She tugged on his butterscotch-streaked hair. "Would you like to run naked on the beach?"

"You're a crazy lady, Amalie Dove."

"Crazy for you, Thomas Jericho. Crazy *with* you."

"Have you forgotten that the island's crawling with reporters who are dying to catch Madame X naked on the beach?"

"I tricked 'em." She tossed her head and laughed. "Ruby's sister, Maggie, put on my clothes and a black wig and let them catch her sneaking out the back on the way to the airport. I put on Maggie's clothes and a red wig and walked out the front with Ruby bold as you please. I've been hiding out in the tree house. Maybe I'll move in."

Jericho's eyes narrowed. "You can't put them off forever."

She nodded wisely. "I know that." Her legs loosened from around his waist and she slid down his body with a luxurious shimmy. "But can we pretend otherwise just for tonight?"

"Pretend?"

"Fantasize, then," she said. "I'm Madame X, remember? You'd better get used to it."

He grinned. "You start."

She closed her eyes for a moment. "This is a story about the loneliest belle on Belle Isle."

"Sounds sad."

"Not entirely." She took his hand and pulled him down into the sand. "The story begins at midnight on the moonlit beach of an obscure little island off the South Carolina coast. A woman walks the beach alone."

"Alone and lonely?"

Amalie paused for a moment to think that over. "Yes," she said gravely. "She doesn't truly acknowledge it, but, yes, she's lonely. Her life is incomplete, so she fills the empty spaces with her daydreams.

"And that's why, when one night she comes across the pirate, she believes at first that he is a figment of her imagination." Amalie picked up Jericho's hand and moved closer to him in the sand. The warmth and solid breadth of his body reassured her that he was no fleeting fantasy. "The pirate is tall and strong and pulsing with vitality. He has long tawny hair that the wind whips across his hard, battle-scarred face...."

"An eye patch?" Jericho asked with a wink.

"No." She gazed into his eyes. "His eyes thrill her. They're like a cat's in the dark—eerily pale, alight with a dangerous glint that speaks directly to the woman's secret yearning to do something wicked."

"Aha. She wants to run naked on the beach."

Amalie laughed softly in her throat and pressed her cheek against Jericho's. His beard prickled her skin; the tiny speckles of sensation blossomed into a rosy blush that spread its warmth down her throat to her breasts. "And she does. They do. They mate like wild animals, naked and hungry, driven by instinct. She is released from all modesty and inhibition."

Jericho looped his arms around her shoulders. "But sex is all he offers her, isn't it? And not even that for very long. He's leaving."

"Yes, that's true. He's led a hard life. He doesn't know how to show his emotions except through sex. That's all he can give her."

"It's not enough. For either of them."

Amalie leaned her head against his arm, a small smile flitting across her lips. "Little does the pirate suspect that he's given more than he realizes. The woman knows that he loves her, even as she stands on the beach and watches him sail away. He never returns— lost and gone forever."

"And the loneliest belle reverts to her repressed life? Haunted by the memory of her lost love as she walks the beach alone every night?"

"Perhaps," Amalie murmured. "And perhaps as she walks she's not haunted, but alive with memory. Her heart races and her body sings. She dances in the sand. The pirate's gift to her is the knowledge that at least once in her humdrum life she has experienced danger, excitement, lust, love. She has *dared*."

Jericho's grip tightened. "You dared, Amalie."

She lifted her head, her bright eyes welling with tears before she blinked them away. "But I'm greedier than the woman in the story. I want to dare for the rest of my life." Her smile flashed impishly at him. "Will you be my pirate, Tom?"

He hesitated for a moment, listening to the rush of the surf and the imaginary thunder of falling rocks. "I'll be your lover. And if you dare to take on a man who's not even sure how a normal family works, I'll be your husband." He answered the mischief of Amalie's expression with a low moan as desire's welcome tendrils twined around his heart. He lay back in the sand, taking her in his arms. "And, okay, maybe now and then over the years we can come here to the beach and I'll be your pirate...."

"Over the years," she said, making it a promise.

He looked up into her trusting face. He'd held back his feelings for so long that their depth and volatility shocked him. Still, he knew that as well as experiencing sorrow and pain there would be joy and laughter and love. While it wasn't always going to be an easy ride, it was certain that Amalie would be with him all the way.

He touched her cheek and pledged, "Over the years."

Maggie Riley's blue tank top was easily stripped off and tossed away. Amalie held her arms up in the wind that sailed off the ocean, her short dark hair lifting at the roots as she straddled him as proudly as a pagan goddess of the sea. "I've decided to accept myself as Madame X," she announced loftily. "I may meet with the media—at my own discretion. Possibly I'll even write another book."

"Your life will change."

She placed her hands on his chest, over his heart, seductively sliding her fingers in between the buttons of his white cotton shirt. "That's okay. I've come to see that I wanted it to even though I didn't know it. I'll be fine as long as I can come home to Belle Isle—and you."

He rolled his head in the sand, acknowledging at last his need to make love to her, not just this once but for the rest of their lives. She opened his shirt and traced her fingernails over his abdomen in tantalizing, spiraling patterns that dipped ever lower. "Glad to know that I didn't ruin your life," he said hoarsely.

"You set me free." She leaned down to kiss him, her mouth hot and open and eager.

Jericho lifted his head to look up and down the dimpled expanse of vacant sand. "On the beach?" He was leery.

She was not. "Naked on the beach."

"Then I think I'd better put my place in East Hampton up for sale and buy this land instead to keep it nice and private."

"Good idea," she said, even though the Dove family already owned it. She unzipped his jeans.

Jericho sucked in deep drafts of the warm salt air. "I can see this is going to be one hell of a marriage."

Amalie looked up and smiled. "It's going to be positively wicked."

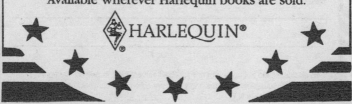

Take 2 bestselling love stories FREE

Plus get a FREE surprise gift!

Special Limited-Time Offer

Mail to Harlequin Reader Service®

> 3010 Walden Avenue
> P.O. Box 1867
> Buffalo, N.Y. 14240-1867

YES! Please send me 2 free Harlequin Temptation® novels and my free surprise gift. Then send me 4 brand-new novels every month, which I will receive before they appear in bookstores. Bill me at the low price of $3.12 each plus 25¢ delivery and applicable sales tax, if any.* That's the complete price, and a saving of over 10% off the cover prices—quite a bargain! I understand that accepting the books and gift places me under no obligation ever to buy any books. I can always return a shipment and cancel at any time. Even if I never buy another book from Harlequin, the 2 free books and the surprise gift are mine to keep forever.

142 HEN CH7G

Name	(PLEASE PRINT)	
Address	Apt. No.	
City	State	Zip

This offer is limited to one order per household and not valid to present Harlequin Temptation® subscribers. *Terms and prices are subject to change without notice. Sales tax applicable in N.Y.

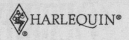

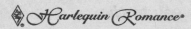

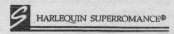

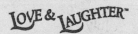

DEBBIE MACOMBER

invites you to the

HEART OF TEXAS

Join Debbie Macomber as she brings you the lives and loves of the folks in the ranching community of Promise, Texas.

If you loved Midnight Sons—don't miss Heart of Texas! A brand-new six-book series from Debbie Macomber.

Available in February 1998 at your favorite retail store.

Heart of Texas by Debbie Macomber

Lonesome Cowboy	February '98
Texas Two-Step	March '98
Caroline's Child	April '98
Dr. Texas	May '98
Nell's Cowboy	June '98
Lone Star Baby	July '98

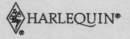

HARLEQUIN®

HPHRT1

MEN at WORK

All work and no play?
Not these men!

July 1998
MACKENZIE'S LADY by Dallas Schulze
Undercover agent Mackenzie Donahue's
lazy smile and deep blue eyes were his best
weapons. But after rescuing—and kissing!—
damsel in distress Holly Reynolds, how could
he betray her by spying on her brother?

August 1998
MISS LIZ'S PASSION by Sherryl Woods
Todd Lewis could put up a building with ease,
but quailed at the sight of a classroom! Still,
Liz Gentry, his son's teacher, was no battle-ax,
and soon Todd started planning some
extracurricular activities of his own....

September 1998
A CLASSIC ENCOUNTER
by Emilie Richards
Doctor Chris Matthews was intelligent, sexy
and *very* good with his hands—which made
him all the more dangerous to single mom
Lizette St. Hilaire. So how long could she
resist Chris's special brand of TLC?

Available at your favorite retail outlet!

MEN AT WORK™

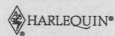 

Look us up on-line at: http://www.romance.net

PMAW2

COMING NEXT MONTH

#693 1-800-HERO JoAnn Ross
Hero for Hire

When Lucas Kincaid agreed to guard the *very* delectable body of
writer Grace Fairfield, he had no idea what lay in store. Someone
wanted the beautiful Grace dead, and the list of suspects was long.
But his biggest challenge was making the woman who wrote about
happy endings believe that Lucas could be the man for her.

#694 THE PRINCESS AND THE P.I. Donna Sterling

Billionaire heiress Claire Richmond had run away to sow some wild
oats, only to realize she wasn't equipped to deal with the "real"
world. Luckily, her cousin sent a detective after her. With strong and
sexy Tyce Walker by her side, Claire had no fear...which only proved
to Tyce what a complete innocent she was, and what a rat *he* was.

#695 SINGLE IN THE SADDLE Vicki Lewis Thompson
Mail Order Men

Daphne Proctor used *Texas Men* magazine to find a husband—and
it worked! She was already half in love with cowboy Stony Arnett
just through his letters. But nothing had prepared her for the
overwhelming chemistry that sizzled between them in person. It
seemed like fate. Until Daphne discovered Stony *hadn't* placed the
ad—and that he had no use for a wife....

#696 SUMMER HEAT Pamela Burford and Patricia Ryan

Sand and surf, romantic sunsets, a house on the beach...and a sexy
stranger to share it all with. What more could you ask from a
vacation? In *July*, uptight Quinn could have lived without mellow
Molly, who showered naked outside and stayed up all night.... In
August, Tom wished Sally wanted him for more than just a passionate
holiday fling, though if that's all he could have.... *Two steamy novels
from two hot authors, together in one very special summer read!*
